I T'S very nice to see you, John," said Ann. "Is all well at Branthorpe?" John paced aimlessly towards the window.

"Oh yes, that is—well, that's what I came to see you about in part. You haven't heard anything then?" he said incoherently, and turned towards her suddenly.

"Heard what?" Ann repeated, puzzled. Surely there could be no change in their betrothal plans again or her father would have been informed.

"It's my brother, he's come home without warning—like a thief in the night."

Ann, of course, was unaware that she had already had a glimpse of the mysterious brother—a glimpse that had quite turned her around.

The
Frensham Inheritance

Audrey Blanshard

A FAWCETT CREST BOOK • NEW YORK

THE FRENSHAM INHERITANCE

THIS BOOK CONTAINS THE COMPLETE TEXT OF
THE ORIGINAL HARDCOVER EDITION.

Published by Fawcett Crest Books, a unit of CBS Publica-
tions, the Consumer Publishing Division of CBS Inc., by
arrangement with Robert Hale & Company

ISBN: 0-449-23557-2

Printed in the United States of America

10   9   8   7   6   5   4   3   2   1

To

MY PARENTS

ONE

ANN DORVILLE continued looking out of one of the tall drawing-room windows of Shipton Grange, although it was some time now since the cortège had passed on its way to the village church. The mortal remains of the sixth Earl of Branthorpe, on their last journey to the Branthorpe family vault, had been drawn by four black-plumed horses, and followed by six carriages together with a goodly number of mourners on foot. Only dark shapes were visible now in the November gloom, but Ann could still see in her mind's eye the mourners' bright flaring torches as they bobbed slowly past the gates and then above the low, newly planted shrubbery which divided the Grange from the village road. Ann stared at the blackness outside, absently fingering the thick gold cord of the curtains.

Her mother looked up from her embroidery frame by the fireside. "You'll catch a chill by that window, my love," she said, in her customary authoritative tones. "It's quite bitter this evening. I do hope your father has consented to ride in one of the carriages."

"I expect Mr. Frensham will see that he does," her daughter replied, as she turned from the window.

"Well, I trust so," Mrs. Dorville said doubtfully, "but if I know anything of your father he will be only too conscious of his lack of consequence as mere neighbours of two years' standing." She peered short-sightedly at her work. "Ring for the lamps to be lit, would you, my love?"

Before settling on the sofa, Ann leaned forward to the braid bell-pull by the mantelpiece. Both ladies wore dark dresses though not full mourning. Ann had spent the past few days stitching black ribbon on to her lilac sarcenet gown, and her mother had on a brown crape with black trimmings.

As the firelight caught her daughter's face, it seemed to Mrs. Dorville that her eyes were over bright. "You mustn't take this too hard, my love, though I own his lordship's death has been a great shock. It was un-looked for in one seemingly so hale, but then he did ride all the way from London in atrocious weather. Just imagine, two days and it never stopped raining once, I collect! It is not to be wondered at that he con-tracted a fatal inflammation of the lungs." She pushed the embroidery frame aside, and looked thoughtfully at her daughter. "It need have no serious effects on your plans, I am sure, if that is what is perturbing you."

"Oh no, I hadn't really considered—that is," stumbled Ann, a little taken aback that her mother should believe her so selfish. "I was thinking about poor Lady Amelia. It must be dreadful for her to lose her father like this when she has scarcely left off wear-ing weeds for her husband."

Prickett came in to attend to the lamps at that mo-ment.

"Yes, for one of such tender years it would seem she has had a wretched time," agreed Mrs. Dorville, al-though her mind, not unusually, was on more personal matters.

Ann blinked her dark lashes rapidly as if against the sudden glare of light. Her normal creamy complexion was faintly flushed and this enhanced her blue eyes. Any claim to real beauty was marred by an over-straight nose, but her countenance had a classic symmetry, emphasised by her smooth centre-parted black hair which was caught up in a chignon. In repose her expression could present to a stranger a slightly forbidding aspect, but her features were quickly transformed when animated by the lively humorous eyes.

"Ah, that's better," Mrs. Dorville said in affected tones, when the lamp shed light on her colourful tapestry. "I'm so glad your father insisted on these new oil lamps, I really don't know how I contrived with candles for so long in our Town house." As soon as the manservant had left her voice reverted to a more normal tone. "As I was saying, my love, I do not consider this unhappy event need make any material difference to the arrangements in hand for your marriage to Mr. Frensham."

"Oh, but mama, there is bound to be a delay now! There will be a period of mourning, and surely the Marriage Settlement will be complicated by his father's death? He's not the eldest son, you know," Ann gently, but unwillingly, reminded her mother.

"I do know, my love," she responded with some acerbity, "and it is a thousand pities that the Settlement was not concluded before his lordship's death. However, I am persuaded that John Frensham was his lordship's favourite son, and it is not to be supposed that the elder brother will get a groat in the circumstances," she concluded, rather obscurely.

Ann looked troubled. "Just because the elder brother is in India surely does not mean that he cannot inherit his father's estate and the title?"

"His lordship would be powerless in the matter of

the title, of course, but I think we shall find that he has
not bequeathed anything further in *that* direction.
There was some family quarrel, as you know, but it
was all before our time," Mrs. Dorville said dismissively. "It would not surprise me to see you mistress of
Branthorpe Park within the year," she confided.
"Naturally, the Dowager will remove to the Dower
House," she said, almost as an afterthought. It had
been a severe disappointment to her to find that her
only child's considerable dowry had not proved sufficient to captivate the attention of at least an heir to a
Viscountcy, but an Earl's indulged younger son was
proving a surprisingly satisfactory substitute.

Ann was not enjoying this conversation, nor had she
spoken quite truthfully when she said that she had not
considered the effect of the death of her future father-
in-law on her marriage plans. For a brief moment, in
fact, a secret hope had been cherished by her that the
wedding might be abandoned altogether. An heiress of
some twenty summers, she had rejected all the
suitable—and many unsuitable—connections so far
proposed for her by her parents. But when the
Honourable John Frensham sought her hand, with the
apparent approval of both families, it had been hard
for her to refuse. None of her well-worn reasons for re-
jection applied. He was not decrepit, being roughly her
own age; he was not repulsive to behold, being of open
countenance and fashionable but not dandified in his
dress; and he was not a blatant fortune-hunter as was
evident from her father's satisfaction with the details of
the proposed Marriage Settlement. It was not a love
match either, but this was an objection which she had
not put forward before, and she did not intend to
present it now. After two London seasons it was surprising, perhaps, that not one of the manifold suitors
produced for her was acceptable, but this was due to

the fact that if they had sufficient rank to impress Mrs. Dorville they were likely to be ageing widowers or bachelors, and if they were young enough to interest her daughter they were scared off by the prospect of such a formidable mother-in-law.

"I think we must wait until the estate has been settled and papa's attorney knows what effect it will have on our Marriage Settlement," Ann said quietly. "For my part I shall be quite content to go with John into Lincolnshire as we planned—if he is still to take possession of Wragston Hall, of course."

"But think, my love, how convenient to be a mere half mile away at the Park! You will be positively *buried* in the wilds of Lincolnshire!" Mrs. Dorville stabbed erratically at her canvas.

Ann smiled. "Only a few days ago you were saying how convenient it would be if I were situated in Lincolnshire, nearer to Town, and away from the wilds of Yorkshire."

"Well now you will have both establishments," retorted her mother impatiently.

"Mama, we cannot know anything for certain yet, and I do not think it right in us that we should discuss it so, when his lordship's funeral is not even over."

"Oh!" she gasped, "I did not think to see the day when my own daughter would tell me how to conduct myself." Then her attention was caught by the sounds of carriages rumbling past the house, at a considerably brisker pace than nearly an hour before. "There! the funeral *is* over," she cried defiantly. "I wonder if your father will go back to the Park for the funeral feast?"

"Oh, I'm sure he will, it would be only courteous in him to do so."

"There will be the reading of the Will, of course, and he won't be concerned with that—not directly in any event," she added gratuitously.

Ann was surprised to learn that the Will should be settled so promptly. "How do you know it is to be read tonight, mama?"

"Oh, it is the custom on such occasions," she stated with conviction. "Whilst all the relations involved are gathered together, you see."

Mrs. Dorville was a commanding-looking woman with a dark mass of curling hair beneath her lace-trimmed cap; even seated her height was apparent. But Ann doubted these confident assertions, knowing that her mother, as a successful wine-merchant's wife and the daughter of an officer in a mere foot regiment, had as little experience of the ways of the nobility as she had herself.

"Well, he has not returned, so it seems he has gone back to the Park," commented Ann presently.

"Yes, I think perhaps we will have a tray brought in here. Your father will not be wanting dinner tonight."

To Ann's relief, when a particularly delicious cold pigeon pie was placed before them, her mother's attention was turned to the accomplishments of the new cook; the only dangerous moment arising when she asserted that it was not to be expected that they could have a French chef in their employ, as they had at Branthorpe Park. She expressed a wish, nevertheless, that Ann would interest herself in the intricacies of French cuisine for future application.

Mr. Dorville returned after the trays had been removed and as the ladies were drinking their tea. He was a well-built man in his early fifties, and this evening looked particularly imposing in his blacks; the face was at odds with the solemn garb, however, being rubicund, as befitted a wine-merchant, and with an inveterate twinkle about the eyes which, even now, was apparent.

"You must be quite chilled to the marrow, Mr. Dorville! Ring for some negus," instructed his wife, while he rubbed his hands together and headed towards a sidetable.

He gave a tolerant smile. "You know very well I abhor hot adulterated wine, m'dear. It's a crime to treat even the stuff you drink in such a manner. No, I will help myself to a cognac."

"As you wish," his wife said petulantly, "although I warrant you have not lacked spirits during the past hour!"

"Oh no! They do not lack spirits at the Park, but his late lordship kept a deplorable cellar! What's the use of a fancy French cook, if you've nothing fit to drink in the house, eh?"

"Mr. Dorville!" exclaimed his wife, affecting outrage. "I vow you speak so only to vex me! It is not fitting to criticise the dead—and our future in-law, too."

Well, he can scarcely be both now, can he, m'dear?" he protested sadly. "This is a wretched business. I cannot believe yet that we have lost our good neighbour. He was a fine man—never condescended me once," he mused, now firmly established with his back to the fire, between the two seated ladies.

"I should hope not!" exclaimed his wife. "You paid him an exorbitant rent for this land and the derelict shell of a building which he dignified with the name Grange. And look at the improvements you have made!"

"All that is quite off the point, m'dear," said Mr. Dorville mildly. "It would not be to everyone's taste to have a parvenu deposit a modern stuccoed dwelling at their ancestral gates—granted that it is designed by an architect who is all the crack!" he conceded to his agitated spouse.

"A parvenu! You pitch it too strong, but I refuse to

be provoked." However, her resolution was unequal to her feelings, and she added: "I trust that in the near future the Park will also have a few improvements. No child of mine will tolerate such primitive surroundings, I vow."

A slightly baffled expression settled on Mr. Dorville's features and Ann decided it was time to change the course of the conversation. "Was it a lengthy oration, papa?"

"Ay, you know Parson Fowler! But it was well done, and there was a mort of people there." He drained his glass and went to sit beside his daughter.

"Mr. Cuffe was at the Park, I presume?" enquired his wife.

"The Branthorpe attorney? No, I understand he was absent on business from his London chambers when news of the Earl's demise was received there."

"Then who read the Will?" she pursued.

"I doubt anyone has read it, though I made no particular enquiry, of course."

Mrs. Dorville looked quite affronted at this evidence of her husband's mismanagement.

"How was Lady Branthorpe?" Ann asked him.

"She behaved magnificently as you would expect, and she was all concern for her daughter, who was looking very whey-faced, poor child."

"We must wait upon them, mama, at the first opportunity."

"I hope I know where my duty lies," was the tart response.

"That reminds me," said Mr. Dorville, "young Frensham begged me to thank you for your condolences, but fears it may be some time before he is free to call upon you. He is fully occupied unravelling his father's affairs, as you may imagine."

"It seems unfair he should have this burden which is rightly his brother's," Ann remarked.

"So it is," her father agreed, "and he is happier astride his horse than casting accounts, I'll warrant you! But for the moment it is quite unavoidable. Assuming a letter was despatched at once to the heir in India, it would be the best part of a year before he could be back in England. And, as it appears he left under some sort of cloud, I would hazard that it is not at all certain he will wish to return."

"Was any reference made to him by the assembled company tonight?" asked Mrs. Dorville.

"Not in my hearing, but then, beyond being referred to as that 'unfortunate business', I've never heard any of the family mention him."

"His sister, Lady Amelia, misses him I think," Ann said. "They were quite close apparently."

Mrs. Dorville brought the conversation firmly back to more practical matters. "If Mr. Frensham is to get the bulk of the estate it is only reasonable he should have the handling of his father's affairs now."

Her husband looked surprised. "How should he get the bulk? I would imagine the estate to be entailed to the heir, although I grant you in the circumstances young Frensham may get a lion's share of the fortune. I can vouch for his father's generous intentions over the Marriage Settlement, but intentions over that count for little now. It does throw a bit of a blight over everything until we know what effect this will have." He turned to his daughter. "If Frensham has been left in the basket, it will mean crying off. Will you mind, kitten?" he asked, genuine concern on his florid face.

Ann shook her head. "No, truly, I like Mr. Frensham well enough, but my heart would not break, I promise you."

Her open expression reassured him. "There's my

good girl," he said, and took up her hand engulfing it in his.

Mrs. Dorville was dismayed. "I see no reason why it should come to that," she said, in rallying tones.

"No, no more do I, my dear," said her husband soothingly. "Now, where's my dinner, eh?"

Ann smiled to herself, while her mother, dismayed for a second time by her spouse, explained that they had partaken of dinner some time before.

" 'Pon my soul, you don't suppose a few foreign sweetmeats at a funeral feast are likely to satisfy me, do you?" He reached for the bell-pull.

TWO

THE COLD morning fog clung persistently about Branthorpe Park, but in spite of this a number of emblazoned carriages had been seen off already from beneath the huge stone porch. The occupants had long journeys ahead of them and wanted to cover as much ground as possible during the short winter hours of daylight.

Fortunately for the Hon. John Frensham, there was no point in lingering outside to speed the parting guests as the last carriage was quickly swallowed up in the misty drive. He was conscious of a decided chilliness as he turned quickly back to the house. He had been compelled to shed his waistcoat these past four days, having none of a suitable funereal hue; his normal taste in these garments tending towards the flamboyant. The rest of his garb on this occasion was unexceptionable: a black superfine double-breasted tail-coat, knee breeches and Hessian boots. Even Aunt Lennox—one of the more trying members of his father's trying family—had found nothing to criticise in his appearance, if little else had been to her taste during the brief visit.

The great studded door was closed quickly by the footman, and smoke billowed out of the cavernous fireplace. No discernible warmth penetrated the lofty hall. Mr. Frensham made haste to his late father's bookroom, where he had earlier caused a fire to be lit.

He found that his mother, the Dowager Countess, had forestalled him; she was seated in a leather wingchair by the fire, a pile of papers on the table by her side. The late Earl, who could not have been called a bookish man, had rarely used the room, and a smell of damp leather bindings pervaded the atmosphere.

"Have they really all departed at last, John? I feared we might be compelled to accommodate some of them for a second night," said the Dowager, who looked very sombre in her black crape.

"I'll not deny it was a close call," he grinned, finding it more amusing now than at the time. "I finally convinced them that it was the proximity of the river which accounted for the denseness of the fog hereabouts."

"I trust you are right! Or we may see them back again before long—and after yesterday, I do not think I could have borne much more." She turned her pale face towards her son. "You were a great help and I am indebted to you, John."

He was embarrassed and looked out of the window although there was little to be seen. In the brief silence which followed they both seemed suddenly aware of their new situation.

John was the first to speak. "I'm sorry it had to be like this, ma'am," he said, in unusually sympathetic tones.

The Dowager waited for him to go on.

"Simon, I mean—and father."

She was touched. "I hardly expected you to understand my feelings about that." She felt a constriction of the throat, familiar during these past few days. "After all you were only—what was it—16? when Simon went to India and you were away at school most of that time anyway." He made no comment, and after a long pause she continued: "Yes, I must own, I always thought they would be reconciled in the end, but never anticipated—" Her voice faded.

"Well, at least father forgave Amelia," John said, in a bracing voice.

"Oh yes," she murmured, "and latterly I think he had forgiven Simon too, but it hardly signified when he was the other side of the world."

There was a moment's silence, then her son asked: "Has Simon ever been told of this change of attitude?"

She detected a slight sharpness in the question and hesitated before replying. "I did write to him about five months ago for the first time. As you know your father forbade any communication with him, but when Amelia came back home after Morley's death she had Simon's direction in India. Your father seemed to be softening in his attitude to his daughter and I could not help hoping that this might come to include Simon too. Yes, I wrote to him of the improved situation here." She sounded very tired.

In fact they were both finding the conversation difficult; neither had discussed Simon before. John enjoyed being the only son, and he barely remembered his brother. Since meeting Miss Dorville he had been interested only in his own future; and there was no doubt that this was rosier while Simon was virtually in exile. His mother understood this very well, but now that her husband was gone, she was more keenly aware than ever of the absence of the rightful heir and her favourite son. She would have given anything to have him here at this moment, but instead she said suddenly: "I wish Cuffe were here—what is the wretched man doing, do you think?"

"God knows!" cried John impatiently, "but I suspect he won't be anxious to travel over 200 miles in this weather—not our cautious Cuffe."

"I could wish Branthorpe had had some of his caution," lamented the Dowager. "*He* would hardly ever take a closed coach. Any more than you will, of course." She looked sadly at her son, who stood silhouetted by the small arched windows.

"No, but I've yet to ride through two days of unceasing rain—and for no reason! It was madness!" The escutcheons in the glass strengthened his oppressed feeling of being in a shrine this particular morning.

"He would have called it resolution—he prided himself on it. That's why he would not yield over Simon."

"But he did, in the end," said John tersely.

The Dowager studied the slight fair figure of her son. He had the misleading appearance of fragility common to her side of the family. Simon favoured his father's more stalwart build; he must be very like him by now, she reflected. She forced her mind back to her present problems.

"I came in here to look for the Will," she told her son, in a business-like tone, aware that this was John's only interest in his father's book-room. "He had a copy made in the year nine when he changed his bequests, depriving Simon of the principal fortune. I recall he was afraid that, because it was unusual, it might not be carried out. He ensured that everyone knew where to look for it—and what a cold fury he was in at the time! You know all that, of course," she said hastily, fearing she would aggravate him with this digression. "The copy should still be here in his desk. Have you looked?"

"Yes, I couldn't wait upon Cuffe's arrival. It hasn't come to light yet."

The Dowager frowned. "That is rather odd." She thought for a moment, then suggested her husband might have taken it to Town with him. "He's had dealings with Cuffe lately about the Marriage Settlement—perhaps he wanted it for that."

"Why should he?" argued her son. "Cuffe has the original, and anyway father merely had to settle an immediate income on me—to help with the upkeep of Wragston. Dorville, bless his prickled heart, provides the rest."

His mother, recalling that the income thus casually referred to, was some three thousand pounds, and was itself in addition to the income from the Wragston estate which he would acquire when he came of age in two months' time, said severely: "I deplore your attitude John! You have been exceedingly fortunate. What younger son has such a settlement, and a truly charming heiress virtually cast at his feet? And I do not scruple to say that, in spite of all this, you have shown a regrettable lack of interest in the practical running of this estate," she added, stung into rash accusations.

Any reference to younger sons, or his lack of enthusiasm for work nettled him; the combination of the two was too powerful to withstand. "I may not be as fortunate as you seem to think if this Will is misplaced!" he burst out savagely. "With my pockets to let do you think Dorville will be anxious to part with either his daughter or her £50,000?"

His mother ignored this outburst. "Perhaps Branthorpe intended adding a codicil, settling something on Amelia?" she hazarded, in an attempt to calm him. "After all, she is quite without means now. Your father did not give her a groat after she left home. It was as well he didn't, in any event," she mused. "It would have run through young Morley's hands in a trice."

John was not listening; he made a sudden decision. "I'm going to see Cuffe! This must be cleared up soon, and I can't kick my heels here not knowing whether I'm a pauper or not."

The Dowager looked taken aback. "You're not going to leave me, John? Just when your father's steward is fussing like a wet hen over everything? I shall be quite overset by his bustling about."

"Nonsense ma'am!" retorted her son briskly. "Featherstone is no match for you and you know it. *He* knows it, I'll warrant, and will be notable for his absence at the moment."

"Then I shall be quite deserted," she complained, telling herself that Simon would not have abandoned her in this shabby manner.

"There's Amelia," he pointed out, "and perhaps I should ride after Aunt Lennox and bring her back? I'll swear that cumbersome coach hasn't jounced her farther than the cross-roads yet."

Disregarding this suggestion, the Dowager made one more attempt to deter him. "Cuffe is most likely on the road here already, you know, you are bound to miss him."

"If he is—and I am far from convinced of it—I shall merely take the opportunity to order some suitable sombre waistcoats, and then return at once," he assured her somewhat flippantly, already enlivened by the thought of activity.

"No, you will not, John," commanded the Dowager, forgetting her helpless role and assuming her autocratic one effortlessly. "If you persist in this mutton-headed scheme you will spend one night at least at Sackville Street and reassure our people that their places are secure. They will be in a state of uncertainty having had no word since the bare news of Branthorpe's death. No!" she said, holding up a black-bemittened hand, "I will brook no argument. In Simon's absence I am head of this family and you would do well to bear that in mind."

John put on one of his sullen looks, but acquiesced. "I collect you have no objection to my bespeaking the waistcoats?" he enquired peevishly.

"Of course not, but I would adjure you to limit your expenditure to what is absolutely necessary, for the moment."

He fired up at this recommendation. "There is no suggestion that I shall lack the means to clothe myself adequately in the future, I trust?"

The Dowager smiled at his petulant expression, reflecting that, save the addition of his rather bushy side-whiskers, it had not changed substantially since he was in leading strings. "Come, John, let us not fall into a dispute at such a time. I am persuaded all will come right for you."

"I wish I had your confidence," he responded mororsely. A thought suddenly occurred to him, and with an altered tone he said: "If the Dorvilles call on you whilst I am in Town, ma'am, you might express the same optimism to them on my behalf."

The Dowager raised her eyebrows. "Surely the subject is hardly likely to be raised during a visit of condolence?"

"If I know my future mother-in-law it will be the principal matter under discussion," John snorted.

His mother smiled to herself, acknowledging the truth of this.

"With your permission, I shall take the chaise," John continued. "Don't stare! I may have to capture Cuffe, and every comfort must be on hand to lure him away."

"Of course, but take Joliffe too," advised his mother, in the hope that the valet would exercise some restraint on her son's behaviour.

There was a gentle scratching at the door and Amelia came into the book-room. The family had become accustomed to seeing her in black in recent months, but custom made it no less unflattering to her. Her small, pretty features seemed quite extinguished by the dismal attire, and her only ornament was a gold locket around her throat. But neither her mourning nor her harrowing experiences served to make her look other than less than her two-and-twenty years.

Her mother welcomed her fondly, but John, after a brief greeting, begged to be excused and strode to the door.

"Oh, I'm sorry, have I interrupted some private discussion?" Amelia asked, turning to go.

"Nothing of the kind, my child," her mother assured her. "It is simply that John cannot wait to quit the Park and its inhabitants."

He made a mild, cursory protest, but took his leave nonetheless.

"Where is he going?" enquired Amelia, as she came towards the fire.

The Dowager raised her hands in a helpless gesture. "The copy of the Will cannot be discovered here and

John has no patience. He is going up to Town to the attorney."

"But Mr. Cuffe is expected here any day, surely?"

"Yes, I am certain of it— he is simply taking his time. However, now I consider the matter I am not altogether sorry that John is going to be absent for a few days. I am beginning to think your father *did* change his Will, and I wish to see Cuffe before John does."

Amelia sighed. "Oh dear, all this has come about because of me! How can I make up for all the trouble I set loose about me?" Her face crumpled, and she brought out from her sleeve a voluminous black-edged handkerchief which was in constant use of late. "And p-poor S-Simon," she hiccupped.

"Amelia!" pleaded the Dowager, with more than a touch of asperity for she had suffered greatly from her daughter's grief and self-reproach in these past months. "I wish you will control these melancholy outbursts, you will merely injure your health and profit no one. Poor Simon indeed! If he had not been as obstinate as your father it would scarcely have been necessary to fly off to the other side of the globe in such a huff."

Amelia made a brave effort and raised her face from her handkerchief. "But if I hadn't compelled him to help me e-elope," she brought out the word with great difficulty, "he would never have defied papa."

"Quit these torments, my child," recommended her parent briskly. "You were exceedingly young and foolish at the time, no one in his senses would dispute that, but Simon was not young, merely foolish, and his guilt was the greater in aiding and abetting you in your addle-pated scheme. *You* have paid for your actions dearly, and need not repine on that count."

"But Simon—" protested Amelia faintly.

"Simon may be living the life of a nabob, and moreover without a single filial responsibility. I cannot but feel he should be indebted to you," her mother informed her bluntly, feeling sudden resentment against her son.

Amelia could not accept this rendering of her brother's exile. "We cannot know, mama! It is a dreadful country—he may have succumbed to a fever. And there are tigers quite near, he said! I wish he were home again, safe."

"Well he is not, and could not be for at least a year, and that is what I want to discuss with you," she added quickly in an attempt to ward off further lamentations. "When did you receive your last letter from him?"

Amelia's fair brows puckered in concentration. "It was in January at my Clerkenwell lodging, and I replied to him from there. That was shortly before I came home."

The Dowager paused, counting the months on her fingers. "Oh, these monstrous delays to the East!" she cried, exasperated. "I calculate he should have received all our letters now, including mine informing him of your return home. However, he may have written more recently to you at Clerkenwell and we must presume that communication lost. I intend to write conveying our melancholy tidings, and pointing out that I expect him to return to Branthorpe at once."

Her ladyship was rewarded by Amelia's first smile in months. "Oh, I'm so glad mama!" The smile faded. "But he may not want to come home if he is as content as you say in India."

"I shall insist," declared the Dowager, confident of her powers of persuasion across several thousand miles of sea.

Amelia looked pensive. "Perhaps he has married," she said. "After all he is five-and-twenty now."

"I am persuaded your disastrous romantical exploits may have cured any tendency he might have had in that direction," her mother commented austerely. "Besides, Cousin Lennox—who secured Simon his appointment with the East India Company, you recall—said that only the most *desperate* mamas shipped out their daughters to India to find husbands. It is not to be supposed that Simon would countenance such a connection." However, in spite of this assertion, the Dowager looked thoughtful.

"Well, then I expect he has taken a native mistress, and he may not want to leave her," Amelia said, forgetful of her audience. "Frederick was used to say—" She caught her mother's eye at this point and further speculation was quelled.

"I will not have that name spoken in my hearing, if you please," she said severely, quite ignoring the aspersions cast on the morals of her eldest son. "Morley's regrettable influence is to be erased from memory." However, her ladyship felt pleased that Amelia was showing signs of her old mischievous spirit; she had used to be such a gay child.

The Dowager changed the subject abruptly. "Tell me, does John confide in you about his forthcoming marriage?"

Amelia gave her mother a questioning look. "Oh no, he never discusses such things with me."

Her ladyship smiled. "Well, it is not to be wondered at if he does not regard you as the ideal confidante in matters of the heart," she said wryly. "Do you think he holds Ann in any affection, or does he simply want Mr. Dorville's franking for his hunters?"

"Oh, I think he must love her mama, she is quite the most charming, kindhearted girl imaginable."

"That, my child, is a complete *non sequitur* and does not signify. I own it would astonish me to see that boy's affections engaged by anything not on four legs, and trust I am right if this marriage must soon be called off."

"But why must it? John will be quite rich now, will he not?"

"He may not be rich enough for Mrs. Dorville's aspirations. You see your father's purpose in altering his Will, when Simon left home, was not particularly to benefit John but to deprive Simon of as much as he could. Consequently, he tied up the bulk of the principal fortune so that it would fall to Simon's heir, and £3,000 of the annual interest from it was to go to John on his marriage. This estate is entailed to Simon of course, but your father has let it run down so, it can scarcely be self-supporting now. I shall do my utmost to hold things together here until Simon returns, but my jointure will furnish little benefit."

"But John has Wragston settled on him when he comes of age, surely?"

"Indeed, but if it should transpire that that is *all* he has settled on him, it will not be acceptable to Mrs. Dorville, I warrant you."

"John wouldn't be able to afford all his hunters then would he?" said Amelia thoughtfully.

"No, and there we have the nub of the matter!" declared the Dowager. "Well we must wait and see what Cuffe has to say to it all."

A feeble ray of sunlight strayed across the bookshelves, illuminating briefly the rich colours of the leather and gilt bindings.

"John was right about the mist, it seems to have cleared. Why not take a walk about the Park, Amelia? You look quite done up with all this brooding indoors. Take Betsy with you. I would come myself but for this letter to Simon which must be written without delay."

Amelia was idly fingering her locket. "Mama," she said in a hesitant, wheedling tone long familiar to the

Dowager, "have I your permission to a little further afield? To Kerswell?"

Her mother looked doubtful for a moment, then seemed to relent. "Very well, but remember you must never take our carriages, even part of the way. I will have no gossip about these visits, so exercise the utmost discretion. Ride there with Betsy, she is the only one you can trust."

"Oh, thank you mama, I knew you would understand." Before she closed the door behind her she said: "Send Simon my best love."

THREE

ONE WEEK later and almost three hundred miles away on the south coast, Mr. Philip Trant also noticed that the morning mist had dispersed—a sea mist in this instance—and decided to take a walk through the steep streets of Lyme. He left his mother's house, a new and moderately sophisticated dwelling with bow windows, contrasting with the humble thatched cottages which made up most of this fishing village. As he strode down the hill to the circulating library, he reflected that it was fortunate that Lyme was becoming slowly popular, or there would be less amenities still in the winter months. True, such smart carriages as there were had left now, and most of the new houses were shuttered, together with the small Assembly Hall, but the library and some recently established modish shops remained open for the use of the few winter residents.

A flurry of dead leaves tumbled past him down the hill and he shivered, drawing his great-coat about him. It was only two weeks since he had stepped off the Indiaman at the London docks, and after nine years in Bengal he was ill-prepared for even the mildest English winter. He was grateful, therefore, that his recently widowed mother had elected to settle in Lyme; she was in possession of an adequate jointure and had rented a neat, comfortable house which suited him well until such time in the near future when he must remove to London. There were fashionable watering places, like Bath and Cheltenham, where many of his Indian colleagues went to recruit on their return to England, but Lyme was not one of these and this made it ideal for his present circumstances.

He walked quickly and was soon inside the library, where a few of the more mature members of Lyme society were benefiting from the fire provided in Mr. Penny's establishment.

On hearing that his new client was the son of dear Mrs. Trant, and recently returned from foreign climes, Mr. Penny, a small round gentleman, became prodigiously animated. Philip explained that he was in search of light, diverting reading matter for a friend who was regrettably housebound at the moment.

While Mr. Penny was selecting suitable volumes for Mrs. Trant and the invalid friend, Philip wandered over to a table where recent magazines and newspapers were displayed. He idly picked up the *London Gazette* and leafed through it. He was just about to relinquish it when his attention was caught by a familiar name, and even Mr. Penny, crackling his wrapping paper, heard Mr. Trant's gasp of surprise; he also noted his customer's changed expression with interest.

Philip hurried over to the counter. "Mr. Penny. I'm sure that in the normal way of things you do not loan your journals, but might I beg of you to allow me to take this home with me for a brief space?"

Mr. Penny, gleefully sensing the excitement of someone else's disaster, said that because it was for Mrs. Trant's son he would certainly waive the regulations in this instance. "Not bad news, I trust sir?" he asked hopefully, as he handed over Philip's bulky package.

"Er—no, no, thank you. That is, I'm not sure—" he said vaguely and in sufficiently distracted tones to satisfy Mr. Penny, even if the details were sadly lacking. Mr. Penny made a mental note to study the *Gazette* minutely upon its return.

Philip bade him a hasty good-day, and hurried home.

His housebound friend, seated strategically in a comfortable chair by the street window, saw Philip approaching, head bent and wide-skirted coat blown open in the freshening wind. "Here's Philip back already Mrs. Trant, and weighed down like a pack mule, by George!" said the friend in some amusement.

Philip's mother, who had a calm rather stately manner about her for all her lack of inches, murmured, "Well now," put down the tray she had just carried in, and went to fetch another glass so that Philip could join his friend in a warming drink right away.

The front door slammed, and a few minutes later Philip came into the parlour, a journal tucked under his arm, with a glass—hastily taken from his mother in the hall—in his hand.

"My dear fellow, you look pinched to death!" exclaimed his friend. "Let me pour you a noggin of your mother's excellent cordial."

Philip approached him, a rather fixed expression on his face, and handed over his empty glass.

His friend busied himself with the decanter, and said quizzingly: "Do I take it that pamphlet is the sum total of reading matter which you have found for me?"

Philip nervously clutched at the rolled up *Gazette* and gave a short laugh. "Oh no, certainly not, I have a veritable mountain of volumes for you." He took an abstracted sip of cordial. "Mm, that's better! It's devilish cold out there I can tell you." He walked over to the bow window, looked out at the street as if it were quite new to him, then stared fixedly into his glass.

In the ensuing silence his old friend observed him with a compassionate eye. "What's amiss, Phil?" he asked kindly.

With a start he looked over his shoulder. "Eh? Oh, do forgive me, you must take me for a bedlamite!" He studied his sick friend's drawn features, and wondered how best to impart the news which he feared might be disastrous for him. "The fact is I picked up this *Gazette* in the library, and—well—there's an item which I think *may* concern you."

"How should it concern me? It seems unlikely enough in all conscience!" He spoke lightly, but Philip thought he detected a certain tension in his manner.

There was a pause while Philip frantically searched for the right words to broach the difficult subject.

"Out with it man! Or Dr. Sandford will take you to task for over-exciting his patient," chaffed the invalid.

"I don't know how to tell you this, but am I right in thinking you have a family in Branthorpe? Yorkshire?" Philip blurted out at last.

His friend cast him a look like thunder. "How in Hades—?" he roared, in amazingly strong accents for a sick man, then, with infinite coldness asked: "How came you to know of this?"

Shattered by the violence of the reaction Philip stammered: "I—it was when you first had the fever in Orissa—you were delirious—oh, you didn't say much intelligible—only Branthorpe, you kept repeating the name Branthorpe." He paused for a moment in great agitation. "Well, I know you have mentioned Yorkshire from time to time," Philip said rapidly, unable to withstand the gaze of disapproval any longer. "So I think you had best read this for yourself." He pushed forward the open *Gazette,* saying, "I fear it may be bad news for you."

Even so, he had not anticipated the grievous effect the few lines of print would have on his friend, whose features, already ravaged by months of fever, became quite grey under the fading sunburn; he stared blindly at the journal.

During the prolonged silence which followed, the grandfather clock sounded in Philip's ears like a blacksmith's anvil; he became alarmed, feeling guilty for bungling the whole wretched business, but was still uncertain what to do.

"What date did we disembark?" asked an expressionless voice without warning.

Startled, Philip echoed: "Disembark? Oh—er, let me see, it must have been the 12th, just over two weeks ago." He studied the fine, dark features of the man before him anxiously.

"The irony of it," he responded in a bitter voice Philip had never heard before, "he died just two days later."

"Shall I leave you?" Philip asked gently, although he could not help thinking that it would be better that his friend should talk.

This question seemed to make the stricken man

aware of his surroundings for the first time in minutes. "Oh, pray forgive me Philip! I am behaving like a boor, and you cannot have the smallest notion of the cause—it is not your fault. I should not have reacted with such ill-temper," he said, full of contrition.

Philip waived these apologies aside. "Then you *are* the son, Simon, er—Viscount Wragston mentioned, I collect? And t-that means you must be the Earl of Branthorpe now," he stammered.

This awed pronouncement seemed to rouse his companion, who looked up at him with a great shout of sudden, surprising laughter. "For God's sake man, do not look so appalled, I beg you! You have been unwittingly nurturing the Viscount Wragston in your bosom these last four years, you know, and you'll not start milording me now, if you please."

Philip was stunned at this confirmation of what he had only half-believed when he first saw the *Gazette* announcement, but he tried to collect his scattered wits. "I am most dreadfully sorry, Simon, to bear such tidings. Would that I had not picked up the wretched paper," he said.

"Please do not reproach yourself on that score. It is better that I should know. The tragic situation I find myself in can only be judged to be my rightful deserts," he stated, and the bitter note had returned to his voice. "You know nothing of my past but it contains very little to be proud of, I assure you."

Philip, not liking his friend's excessive pallor, asked if there was anything he could get for him. "More cordial perhaps, or brandy?"

Simon accepted the cordial from him mechanically, and Philip went to a chair opposite, reflecting that all he had known of Simon was that he had insisted upon an out-of-the-way place to recruit his strength when they arrived in England, and Lyme had met with his approval.

The two men, although both had dark, over-long hair for the fashion of the moment, appeared to have little else in common. Philip at two-and-thirty, seven years Simon's senior, looked the younger at present. His nine years in the Indian heat had not caused him to shed every ounce of spare flesh as it so often did; he still had a round face and, although taller than his mother, gave the impression of a stocky, well-built man. By no means handsome he had, nevertheless, an attractive, benevolent countenance, and this was due largely to his dark lustrous eyes; a feature which, years ago, had earned him the name of "Spaniel" from his schoolfriends at Harrow. When he first met Simon in Calcutta he had admired the tall, elegant young man who had been sent to work in his department of the East India Company.

Simon, only four years later, no longer looked young nor, indeed, elegant. His face, which was still handsome in spite of the premature lines about his grey eyes, had a long stubborn jawline and a sensitive mouth which could look hard—as it did now.

There was silence in the small room, and Philip thought how extraordinary it was to be sitting there with this aristocratic guest, who should by rights have charge of his family estates, yet Simon had never spoken in India of any family.

The clear trilling cry of the milkmaid's voice in the street below, made both men glance towards the window. Her clogs echoed on the cobbles as she walked slowly down the middle of the narrow street, carrying the milk in pails hanging from a yoke across her shoulders. She was stopped presently by a maidservant from a nearby house. Her attractive face was turned towards them as she filled the servant's pitcher with milk.

"I had a sister as comely as that," Simon said quietly.

"Had?" prompted Philip, curious now about his friend's background.

"Who knows? She was the only member of the family to keep in touch with me, and with the least reason, I suspect. I served her very ill." He drew a hand across his brow. "The last letter, almost a year ago, came from her Clerkenwell lodging—yes! Well you may stare. I had to read between the lines but there seemed little joy in her life with the wretch of a husband I helped her run off with."

"I begin to understand, I think," said Philip who was watching him keenly.

"Which is more than I can say at this distance!" Simon mourned, shaking his head. "I must have been incredibly lack-witted. Amelia—my sister—was a love-sick young girl when I last set eyes on her. It had been arranged that she should marry old Andover's heir—a dull, worthy lad admittedly, but she had eyes only for a dandified fellow she'd met in London. I knew very little about him, but if Amelia wanted something in those days I would hazard anything that she might have it. So when she asked for my assistance to elope, I never hesitated."

"Could they not have been apprehended later, and the marriage prevented?"

Simon pulled a wry face. "I am an obdurate dolt—as you have no doubt had cause to reflect from time to time—and wild horses would not have dragged their destination from me. Of course, it was not to be supposed that my father would tolerate such flouting of his wishes, and I saved him the task of turning me off with the proverbial penny by never returning home. I put the maximum distance between us as soon as I could."

"Yes, you made a pretty thorough business of that,

too," murmured Philip, who had quite forgotten now that he was addressing the Noble Earl of Branthorpe.

But Simon paid no heed; he was feeling a certain relief at being able to talk about his family at last. In India it had been easy to put them out of mind, except when, on very rare occasions, Amelia's letters had disturbed his peace.

"Philip, you're a sensible fellow, what am I to do?" entreated his lordship.

"Do?" echoed Philip, who still felt bemused and incapable of bestowing advice on anyone. "Well, you must recover your health and strength before there is talk of doing anything," he recommended.

His lordship's slim fingers gripped the chair arms. "Ay, this damnable fever has left me as weak as a rat."

"It must be remembered that you are fortunate to be alive," Philip told him. "When we set sail from Bengal I had little hope of seeing you survive the voyage, instead of which it did you inestimable good."

"True! I am an ingrate, Phil," cried Simon. "But for your care on that endless journey I would not be here, and you are quite right to remind me of it."

"Well, it was providential I was able to return home at just that moment," Philip was saying, when the door opened quietly and his mother came in to enquire what Mr. Frensham wanted on his luncheon tray.

To Philip's surprise Simon said he would join them at table, and from that moment he made a determined effort to recover. On the voyage from India Philip had been aware that, although his companion was improving slowly, there was a certain spirit lacking in him, as if he had no wish to be better. He realised now that it must have been so, for what had been waiting for Simon in England in the circumstances? He would surely have been compelled to leave these shores again as soon as he had completed his anonymous convalescence?

Mrs. Trant had not been told of the identity of her guest, but Simon was worried that the news would leak out somehow and become common knowledge in Lyme—and then perhaps in London. Philip thought this the exaggerated fear of an invalid but he *was* worried about another matter. He had pondered upon his conversation with Simon and a question had arisen which he wished to put to his friend, but he hesitated to revert to the subject again.

His opportunity came three days after the original discussion when the two men had finished a game of backgammon and were sitting in the half-light from the fire.

"Simon?—I hope you will forgive me raising the subject again, but I feel I must—"

His friend cut across this preamble. "If you refer to my abysmal affairs I shall think it very good in you to take an interest. I own that none of my deliberations these past days seem to much purpose."

Philip by now could distinguish only the white cravat, cuffs and nankin pantaloons of his companion and this suited him very well, for he was uncertain of the reaction his question would bring. "When you spoke of your sister's elopement you said she was young, but did not, I think, mention her age at the time. Do you recall it?"

"Well of course I do! She is about four years my junior and was barely eighteen at that time."

"And was the destination, which you refused to reveal, over the border?"

"Over the border?" Simon reiterated drowsily. "I don't follow your lay, old fellow."

Philip had been afraid he would not; he spelled it out for him. "She was under age, Simon, and could not have married in this country without permission—only in Scotland."

There was a brief silence. "Oh God, what a fool I've been! Even worse than I imagined!" he cried, fully awake now. "But they were married, I'll swear. Morley had a parson on hand and I drove Amelia to meet them both in Huntingdon. When I wrote to her later she had dropped her title, of course, as I had, and called herself Mrs. Morley."

"Well, your sister's age must have been falsified or—" Philip hesitated, "perhaps Morley was abetted by a friend masquerading as a parson for the occasion—it has been known."

Simon stared at his friend for a time. "So," he said at last, "it seems I made a complete bungle of even that! The dandified Frederick must have hoaxed us both. He was all of five-and-twenty and very worldly wise; I was just down from Oxford—but no excuses! I should have consulted someone else or refused to listen to Amelia's pleading altogether. But she was so unhappy and it seemed obvious to try and help her. I had no interest in marriage on my own account and knew nothing of minors—it never occurred to me."

"It would not have occurred to me but for the fact that Mary was under age when we married, and we needed her parents' permission for the wedding before we left England." Philip rarely mentioned his wife, dead these past four years, but he was anxious to say anything which would make Simon blame himself the less at the moment.

"Thank you for your kindness Phil, but nothing can excuse me." Frowning, he went on, "But I can't believe Amelia would have lied about her age—although she *was* infatuated," he conceded, then leaned forward in his chair suddenly. "No, I think you may be right. A counterfeit parson is all of a piece with Morley's conduct. I must find her if she's not legally wed, Phil! God knows, it's too late to mend her reputation, but I'll swear she must be unhappy with such a rogue." He sighed and rubbed a hand across his forehead. "Phil, I am sure you will understand the burden all this is to me. There is no question now, I must go to London right away."

Philip's immediate reaction was to protest, but he did understand so said quietly instead: "Yes, I am persuaded that would be the best course. I make one condition only, and that is that I accompany you."

"Thank you, I do not deserve such a friend," said Simon humbly.

"Well," declared Philip, in an attempt to lighten the tone of this solemn discourse, "we shall both be at a nonplus in Town after such a long absence, I'll warrant you! I for one will be glad of a companion."

Whereupon he put a taper to the fire and lit the candles, and plans were discussed for their early departure.

FOUR

Since John Frensham's departure from Branthorpe Park his mother had given orders for a fire to be kindled in the book-room every morning. It had quickly been borne in on her ladyship that until Cuffe came to her rescue, most of her mornings were destined to be spent in consultation with Featherstone.

Thus almost a week after John had left for London, and the same morning that her eldest son in Lyme first heard of his father's death, Lady Branthorpe awaited the inevitable appearance of the harassed steward. It was while the Dowager was re-reading a letter which had arrived that morning from John, and was hoping—not with any great confidence—that he was behaving with the dignity required of a recently bereaved son, that Featherstone came in. She noted with sinking spirits that he carried a particularly large sheaf of papers under his spindly arm.

The steward was stricken in years for he had served both the fifth and sixth Earls of Branthorpe with devotion; but the servitude had taken its toll and he appeared to have shrunk markedly in the process, both spiritually and physically.

The Dowager, although exasperated by his subservient manner, felt a certain compassion for him, having had some little acquaintance over the years with the Frensham temper and its effects on others. "And what insuperable difficulties face us this morning, Featherstone?" she enquired in a kind enough voice, but her appearance in widow's peaked cap and voluminous black draperies had its usual crushing effect on the steward.

"Em—em, a vast number of bills have been sent on from Sackville Street, m'lady. I had not the least suspicion of their existence," he quavered.

"Add them to the pile," commanded the Dowager wearily. "There is little I can do, having no power of attorney yet. They must wait upon Mr. Cuffe's arrival like the rest of us." Her voice faded as her gaze rested upon the uppermost paper. "One hundred and ninety-nine pounds, ten shillings and one penny," she read out grimly, "to Samuel Hobson, Long Acre, for travelling coach." She regarded the unhappy Featherstone. "This, I presume, is the coach which Mr. Frensham has taken to Town."

"Yes, m'lady," he murmured apprehensively. "I know it is some time since we took delivery—"

"Some time!" cried the Dowager, "it is all of two years."

"Quite so, m'lady. His late lordship had a method, you understand, for what he termed the cattle accounts. In time this came to include coaches and everything connected with the stables, however remotely," he said in a helpful manner.

"Method!" the Dowager exclaimed. "Not notable for its success, I collect," she added dryly.

"Spasmodical, m'lady, if I may say so," he informed her. "His lordship relied heavily on his winnings at the races for the settling of such accounts. I remember it worked splendidly in the year nine," he said, a nostalgic look in his rheumy eyes, "we had a run of winners at Newmarket. It was then the Method was born; his lordship decided that it would be an admirable economy in future to pay *all* his stable expenses from his winnings on the turf."

"I see, and has any account been settled since that halcyon year?"

"Oh yes, indeed," responded Featherstone, in shocked accents. "His lordship was most scrupulous in handing over all his winnings for the purpose—regardless of his losses."

"Well, we must be thankful for that," said the Dowager trenchantly.

The steward gave a little cough. "If I may be permitted to say so, m'lady, his late lordship's Method was a notable improvement on the fifth Earl's arrangements. On his passing over, I recall, almost the entire expenses for the previous ten years were found to be outstanding."

The Dowager, who had heard many tales of her father-in-law's dealings with the tradespeople, reflected that amazingly Featherstone must have welcomed her husband as an easy man by contrast—although he had still been subject to the notorious Frensham Outbursts, common to father and son.

Not wishing to get embroiled in a discussion of family failings with the steward, she took up John's letter again. "Mr. Cuffe, I am informed this morning by my son, is marooned in the West Country visiting a client and has very inconsiderately developed the influenza. So it appears that we may wait some time yet upon his arrival here."

"I'm sorry to hear that, m'lady. There will be a prodigious tangle for the gentleman to unravel when he does come," forecast the steward morosely.

"Well, it is only to be expected that every Tom, Dick and Harry will render his accounts when a death occurs. I am persuaded that there will be no insurmountable problem in settling everything satisfactorily," she assured him, thankful that on the distaff side of the establishment Mrs. Pringle, the housekeeper, would not tolerate her mistress falling behindhand with *her* accounts; that upright lady, she was convinced, would as lief quit the Park.

As soon as the steward had returned to his own office in the west wing, the Dowager repaired to the morning room, intending to have a few quiet words with her daughter. She considered the present funereal atmosphere of Branthorpe to be having a depressing effect on Amelia's spirits.

Lady Amelia was in the morning room, a small solitary black-clad figure, her golden head bent close over more sombre stitchery. This gloomy picture confirmed the Dowager in her resolve. She greeted her daughter warmly and bade her put aside her sewing. "I wish to talk with you, my dear," she said.

Amelia gladly left her work by the window and came to a chair nearer the fire. "Yes, mama, what is wrong?" she asked.

"There now," cried the Dowager triumphantly, to the surprise of her daughter, "if that does not prove I am correct! I vow you have quite despaired of anything being right ever again. True, it is scarcely to be wondered at, but I think it would be a very good scheme if you were to get away from here for a month or two."

"Oh no, mama," protested Amelia in a small voice which the Dowager chose to ignore.

"Your Aunt Digby wrote to me last week and suggested that you stay with them at Bath. They have hired a house there while your uncle takes the waters. Oh, I know it is no longer the season, but that does not signify as you would be unable to dance or visit theatres for a few months yet, in any event. There would be concerts though," she said, warming to her subject, "and Aunt Digby would arrange a few private dinner parties; her two girls are there and I am persuaded it is the very thing to restore your spirits."

"But truly mama, I am quite content to stay here with you. After the last few years I *never* want to leave home again," she said earnestly, her face clouding over at the memory.

"I do understand my dear, but you are still young and must think of starting a new life for yourself."

"That is not possible mama," Amelia protested hotly. "You know it is not! *Everyone* has heard of my squalid escapades, and if you still think to discover an eligible *parti* for me I wish you will not squander your time."

"It may be as well to allow a little time to pass before you think of marriage," she conceded, "but your unfortunate past will soon be a nine day's wonder you know. In any event, there is no call to become a recluse. The diverting company of a few young people would do no harm."

"No, mama," said Amelia firmly, two spots of high colour on her cheeks. "I wish to stay here."

"I am not deceived of course," said the Dowager quietly. "It is your occasional visits to Kerswell which hold you here. Well, they cannot continue for ever you know. I was foolish ever to permit them at all." Then, when she saw the stricken look on Amelia's face, she knew that she had had no alternative but to allow the visits; nevertheless they must be stopped soon and a visit to Bath was the obvious answer. *A few new interests and who knew what may happen?* The Dowager prepared to state her case more persuasively when the butler came in.

"Mrs. Dorville and Miss Dorville to see you, m'lady," pronounced Stagg. The disapproval in his voice was detectable only to those who knew him well.

The Dowager was inclined to tell Stagg to deny her, but decided that it would be good for Amelia to see Miss Dorville, and she might prevail on them to support her in her Bath scheme; she had to bear in mind John's interests too, so reluctantly she instructed the butler to show them in.

Mrs. Dorville advanced upon the Dowager with a curiously compressed smile which it seemed she thought fitting for a visit of condolence. She was expensively clad in a new-looking purple silk walking dress trimmed about the bodice and wrists with sable; an ornate high-crowned bonnet completed the ensemble and emphasised her height. The Dowager swiftly surmised that demi-mourning had run her neighbour into a deal more extravagance than her own weeds.

Amelia rose to greet the visitors and, when the formal expressions of sympathy were completed, she took Ann Dorville to the sofa whilst the Dowager conversed with Mrs. Dorville.

Ann had a matching pelisse over her lilac gown, and a pretty black-trimmed bonnet. She was taller than Amelia, and this morning, with cheeks glowing from the walk across the Park she quite outshone Amelia's more fragile beauty. The two girls had met only occasionally before because, although Amelia had returned home some time in the previous winnter—so John had told her—Ann had not seen her until June. All Ann knew of her was that she had married against the wishes of her family and after her husband's sudden death had returned home to them. She noticed that Lady Amelia wore no wedding ring on her finger now, but had a locket round her throat containing a curl of brown hair.

She asked Amelia about her brother John, although aware that her mother would be exhausting the same topic with the Dowager, as this was her express purpose in coming. Ann had spent a trying week since the Branthorpe funeral as no word had been heard from the Park, and her mother's speculations had grown wilder every day.

Very tentatively Ann suggested that Amelia might like to accompany her now and then on her morning ride.

"Oh that is most kind of you," replied Amelia, delighted. "I confess to being but a poor spectacle on a horse though, and you are a capital hunter, I hear. John speaks of your horsemanship in the most enthusiastic terms."

Whilst quickly disclaiming any extraordinary talents

on the hunting field, Ann thought rather ruefully that riding was the only aspect of a female that Mr. Frensham was likely to judge worthy of comment. "I merely thought that a half hour's trot when the weather is fine would be very pleasant," Ann said reassuringly.

"Oh indeed it would, I shall look forward to it."

Lady Amelia's words were interrupted by the Dowager's voice from across the room. "Well, Miss Dorville, so you have a twenty-first birthday shortly."

Ann felt ready to sink; she had adjured her mother not to broach the subject of her coming of age celebrations during this visit, feeling it most unfitting in the circumstances. The anniversary fell the following month, December, and she was resigned to the plan for a quiet dinner party marking the occasion instead of the ball originally projected by her mother. Ann guessed she had not been able to resist reminding the Dowager of her daughter's imminent fortune which would fall to her on her birthday. Ann blushed for her and stammered something in reply to Lady Branthorpe, and added hastily: "We thought just a small company to dinner, ma'am, would be the most conformable in the circumstances."

"Humbug, my dear!" said the Dowager, so robustly that even Mrs. Dorville's sensibilities seemed affronted. "I would not countenance our bereavement throwing such a blight over your affairs. You must have your ball, and I am persuaded that John might be permitted to lead you in the first dance too."

Ann was a little disappointed because she knew that Amelia would feel excluded from the celebrations, not being allowed to dance, but she had to own that for herself she would prefer a ball. In spite of that she resolved to try and hold to her plans for a dinner party, although it would not be easy now that her mother had been given *carte blanche* by the Dowager.

Mrs. Dorville, having accomplished her mission satisfactorily, extended a black-gloved hand to the Dowager, and the two visitors took their leave.

The Dowager had been pleased, at the time, of the diversion created by Miss Dorville's anniversary, for it had turned the talk from John's expectations. However, she recognised now that her Bath scheme was doomed to failure for the moment, due to the celebration of this event; but she was mollified to see that Amelia appeared quite animated by the visit and was talking of future outings with Miss Dorville.

So, to Amelia's vast relief, the Bath visit was not reverted to again.

FIVE

PHILIP TRANT had been unable to persuade his mother that it was necessary for him and his friend to remove to London at such short notice. She did not believe her son's protestations that he must call so soon upon India House where he had been promised a post. Convinced that poor sick Mr. Frensham would, at the least, take a fatal chill from the chaise journey to London she pro-

vided him with every imaginable comfort, from rugs
and cordial to a small chest of specifics and a hot brick
for his feet.

In the event the two friends arrived in London, without incident, four days after Simon's decision to find
his sister. At the hotel in Vigo Lane, near Piccadilly,
Simon let Philip make the preliminary enquiries whilst
he paid off the post boys. It had been decided that as a
precaution Simon would use the name French for the
time being.

Over a meal in their private sitting-room the pair
discussed their immediate plans. "First of all I must
make enquiries at the house agents for a suitable lodging. As soon as I can find something you must move in
with me, of course. It will be safer for you than any
hotel," said Philip, tucking into a platter of mutton cut-
lets. "Mm, this is a vast improvement to be able to
taste a bit of English mutton instead of Lord-knows
what with curry."

His lordship, who had been responsible for the in-
stallation of the French chef at Branthorpe, agreed in a
half-hearted fashion, and reverted to the subject of
lodgings. "I mislike imposing on your good nature in
this way, Phil, but cannot deny it would be mighty convenient to be incognito for a while."

"That's settled then," said Philip quickly, before any
objections could be raised. "I must say it is a blessing
the shops are open all hours. It will be quite five
o'clock before we are ready to leave," he said consulting his fob watch.

"My prime need is for some respectable warm clothing, but I cannot approach my old tailor, of course,"
said Simon, looking gloomily at his inadequate Indian
silk tailcoat. His boxes were still at the docks until his
future was settled. "Well I must contrive to purchase

what I may, where I may, but trust I will not be compelled to sink to the Monmouth Street level!"

"Heaven forbid!" laughed Philip. "It would not be the thing for a noble Earl to sport cast-off duds." He spoke lightly, but regretted his clumsiness when he saw Simon's fleeting expression. "Sorry—stupid of me," he mumbled.

"Gammon, Phil! I must learn not to show so much sensibility about my absurd situation," Simon said contritely.

Philip left the hotel first, while his friend was still hesitating whether or not to venture forth without an extremely ill-fitting and unflattering great-coat borrowed from Phil. Caution won the day over vanity, for he decided he could ill-afford to contract a severe chill at the moment.

Feeling too embarrassed to ask the doorman to summon a hackney for him, he hurried across the seemingly vast carpeted hall to the door.

"Simon! Is it really you? How absolutely amazing!" shrieked a feminine voice behind him.

With sinking heart he turned to verify his suspicions. "Miss Merivale," he murmured in tones significantly lacking in enthusiasm. He had to be grateful for her familiarity as it meant only his first name had been shared with any onlookers.

Clarissa Merivale approached him dramatically from the foot of the stairs, extending a slim gloved hand. His lordship, more acutely aware of his beggarly appearance every minute, felt quite ludicrous bestowing a cursory kiss on the member, thinking crossly that only Clarissa would demand such an outmodedly demonstrative greeting.

As she babbled on about how prodigiously surprised she was to see him, and he interjected suitable responses, his only instinct was to escape as soon as possible.

Miss Merivale was the daughter of the Surveyor-General of the East India Co. in Orissa, and had spent several years there, theoretically under the surveillence of her one surviving parent, until she secured a husband. The various candidates for this honour quickly discovered that Miss Merivale's favours were readily available without resorting to the dire measure of matrimony. Simon, although never a serious contender for Clarissa's hand had, during his first despairing months in India, sampled those favours. Since then, he suspected, she had never quite given up hope of becoming Mrs. Frensham; he hazarded that her feminine intuition, aided by considerable experience, shrewdly told her that he might be more eligible than appearances suggested.

Conscious of the eyes of various hotel minions upon them, he decided, as an initial precaution, to escort Miss Merivale outside. She was dressed in a pink velvet carriage-costume and carried a huge fur muff. At one time no mean expert on the subject, his lordship was now lamentably out of touch with current feminine modes, but his instinct told him with tolerable certainty that Miss Merivale's ensemble would have been more fitting on a damsel ten years her junior, and one preferably without her red hair.

"I have just this minute arrived in Town, Miss Merivale, and regret I am obliged to dash away, but would be delighted to carry you to your destination. I collect you were just setting forth?" He delivered this damping speech with creditable suavity, whilst propelling her by the elbow to the door. It was then borne in on him that he had made a rash offer; he was travelling by hackney.

As Clarissa accepted his offer, saying she was visiting a friend in Berkeley Street, not far away, his lordship, now standing with her outside the hotel, endeavoured to explain about the hackney. "I had quite forgotten I have no phaeton at the moment, and I regret it would not be the thing at all to accompany you in a hackney."

Miss Merivale's tinkling laugh rang out, further aggravating his worn nerves. "How sweet of you Simon, but I vow *my* reputation will not suffer a decline if yours will not."

He was past worrying about anything as nebulous as his reputation in the present difficulties, and promptly commissioned a hopeful urchin to find him a hackney. He wondered irritably why an hotel which prided itself on gentility had to burn enough flambeaux on its facade to rival the illumination at Vauxhall Gardens: he felt mercilessly exposed to the scrutiny of the many fasionable passers-by. In an effort to conceal his features he bent his head as if to hear Clarissa better.

It was a mistake. Clarissa was quite enraptured by such attentions and clung lovingly to his arm. The hackney carriage arrived after an eternity, and he recklessly thrust a shilling in to the astonished urchin's grubby hand. He told the jarvey. "Berkeley Square" on Clarissa's instructions; understandably she did not want to be seen arriving with him at her Berkeley Street destination.

Simon settled himself somewhat gingerly in the cab; he would scarcely have believed it credible that he should welcome another coach journey that day; he had fully intended to walk, having had a surfeit of rattling about like a dice in a box.

In the dark intimacy of the cab Clarissa snuggled up to him, and said in conspiratorial tones, "What does all this signify? Are the Runners after you? Or the bailiffs perhaps?"

"You always did possess a fevered imagination, Miss Merivale," he said crushingly. "I confess to not looking my best, but I have just arrived from India and lack suitable clothing. I am in search of a tailor at this moment," he said, uncomfortably aware of his unshorn locks curling about his neck; he should have trusted the hotel barber to trim them.

She turned disbelieving eyes upon him. "Well, you cannot have arrived this week, there was no Indiaman docked," she retorted smugly.

Confound her close links with the Company, he thought. "If you must be pedantic about it, I have been here three weeks, but due to illness this is my first opportunity to buy clothes. Does that satisfy you?" he asked, although he was careless of what she thought and only anxious to get this journey over.

"We-ell, I suppose it does explain why you are wearing your brother's great-coat—" she said reluctantly.

"Brother? What do you know of any brother?" he said snappishly, galvanised by the unlooked-for reference to John.

"Nothing, nothing at all," she responded with apparent innocence. "Should I?"

"It is Mr. Trant's coat—I think you have met him, he was with me in Bengal," he said distantly, aware that he was bungling this encounter, but it had been totally unexpected and he was feeling very weary. He had feared meeting his English friends, but had not anticipated the appearance of any from India. Her next remark did nothing to reassure him.

"Of course I am acquainted with Mr. Trant," she said, sitting upright, her hands tucked primly into her muff having sensed a general chill in the atmosphere. "Indeed, I saw *his* name in the hotel book, but was curious to know who Mr. French could be? That must be you, I collect?" she said slyly, looking sidelong at him under long sandy lashes.

He groaned inwardly, wondering if his luck would ever change. "French?" he reiterated, assuming a puzzled air. "I have not the smallest idea what you are talking about. Mr. Trant supplied the names and it must be supposed that he was mis-heard." *Dammit, would they have to remove to another hotel tomorrow?* "I take it you arrived shortly after us this afternoon?"

"I suppose I must have," she said archly, "but I am only engaged to stay there for tonight, unfortunately."

For a panicky moment he wondered if her presence there was not a coincidence, but it could scarcely be anything else, he told himself severely, for their destination had been quite unknown to anyone else.

"I am persuaded my friend, whom I was visiting now, will accommodate my maid and myself tomorrow," Clarissa went on.

He was relieved to hear she had a maid accompanying her; he had feared she was lost to all sense of propriety. The wretched girl must have been abandoned at the hotel, he presumed.

The hackney was slowing down now, and Clarissa was deprived of further opportunity to quiz him about his behaviour. His lordship handed her down. "I will gladly escort you to your friend's house, but I am persuaded my deplorable appearance augurs against it," he remarked hopefully.

Clarissa appeared to struggle briefly between the opportunity to satisfy her curiosity further, and the fear that she might be seen in the company of such a ruffian. "Thank you, it is but a step from here, and there is not the smallest need to accompany me." She smiled sweetly, and went on: "Of course, I shall take my leave of you in the morning before I quit the hotel." Thus she managed to reconcile both snobbery and curiosity to her satisfaction.

Simon bade her a stunned goodbye, and stood by the

hackney gloomily watching her departing figure until startled by the jarvey's voice. "What now, Guvnor? I ain't got all night."

His lordship felt too unnerved now to walk the London streets, and he asked the driver to take him to the nearest tailoring establishment. The jarvey made a fortunate choice and within the hour Simon was back in his hotel warmly—if unfashionably—clad. He strode more confidently across the hotel entrance hall this time, although alert for the reappearance of Miss Merivale, and trod the stairs to their rooms. He found the sitting-room snug with the fire nicely ablaze, and the curtains closed, and as Philip had not yet returned he sat and dozed.

It lacked about half an hour to midnight when Mr. Trant came back and woke him. Simon thought his round face looked a little pale with fatigue, but he was clearly cheerful about something.

"Well, I do believe I've found something for us already," he said, peeling off his gloves. "Quite near, in Clifford Street."

His lordship searched his memory of London's geography and recalled that it was a little farther from the Branthorpe house in Sackville Street than this hotel, and decided it would serve. "You cannot know what a relief it is to hear that. It would not be possible to take possession at first light tomorrow, I collect?" he asked his friend, with the suspicion of a twinkle in his grey eyes.

Philip stared at Simon. "You've not been ferreted out so soon?"

Simon nodded over interlaced fingertips. "Miss Clarissa Merivale, no other."

"Good God! Where?"

"Here! In the next room for all I know," Simon informed his astonished friend. "From my point of view, of course, it could have been worse. At least she only knows my recent Indian past and is quite unaware of my Branthorpe connections. Nevertheless, I think the lady's suspicions were definitely aroused." He laughed. "It is scarcely to be wondered at! I behaved like a gudgeon, looked like a scarecrow—and all under the guise of the mysterious Mr. French!"

"She's seen the hotel book, as well then?" concluded Philip. "Of all the ill-luck." After a pause, he chuckled and said: "She has been endeavouring to fix your interest for years of course!"

"I know it!" cried his lordship ruefully.

"She could not conceivably have been aware of your presence here, could she?" asked Philip, with a worried frown.

"No, I am certain of that. However, that young lady may well have known of my arrival in this country. I am persuaded she studies the Indiaman arrival lists closely, on the catch for returning nawabs who eluded her in India no doubt."

"Young lady!" roared Philip with uncharacteristic violence. "Four-and-thirty I would hazard at my most charitable."

"Tut-tut," chided his lordship, "where's your chivalry?"

"Absent where Miss Merivale is concerned, I fear," retorted Philip cheerfully. "But don't worry," he said, reverting to the original topic, "I can take possession of the new lodgings tomorrow afternoon."

"That's splendid news, but certainly I must be gone from here betimes in the morning—long before Miss Merivale stirs, in any event. I intend to seek out my sister's lodging, and will join you at Clifford Street later in the day. Oh, and I beg of you not to breathe a word of your new address should Clarissa accost you, as I am persuaded she will!"

"You may depend on me for that," Philip assured him, with considerable feeling. He went to the closet to hang up his coat. "There's the devil of a queer smell in here—perfume or something," he remarked, sniffing.

"Ah yes," said his lordship airily, "I fear that's the ubiquitous Clarissa again; she clung to your coat like a limpet in the hackney, as I recall."

"Well, really!" expostulated his friend. "I could wish you had taken my advice to stay in and rest this evening."

"I am at one with you there, my dear fellow," agreed his lordship dryly.

*   *   *

By nine o'clock the next morning Simon was in Clerkenwell and had made enquiries at his sister's lodging only to be told by a slatternly landlady that Mrs. Morley had left a twelve month ago. As for Mr. Morley it seemed he had died suddenly shortly before Amelia's departure. Simon had great difficulty in obtaining this information as his informant was, even at that early hour, well primed with gin, but he believed her when she told him she had no knowledge of Mrs. Morley's present whereabouts: Amelia would scarcely have confided in such a woman.

His hopes crushed by this unexpected news, Simon wandered aimlessly about the city streets until, hours later, he found himself near Cuffe's Chambers. Of course, Simon thought, the family attorney was the man to approach. Perhaps Amelia herself had turned to him for help?

His lordship's pace quickened and, heedless of the consequences of revealing his presence in the country to the attorney—for he knew the Branthorpe estate was entailed upon him and complications would inevitably ensure—he rushed up the dingy stairs. He soon discovered, from an indolent clerk, that Mr. Cuffe was absent in Somerset and although his return was imminent he would be leaving again at once on further business. The clerk displayed clear disbelief when Simon announced he was the Viscount Wragston, and he decided nothing would be gained by arguing with the lad. He left, but resolved to return early the following morning and stay there till Cuffe appeared.

It was five o'clock when Simon finally sought out Philip in the new Clifford Street lodgings, having visited earlier a tailor—of more distinction than the jarvey's choice—and bespoken such mourning apparel as he suspected might be necessary in the near future. Philip told him that Miss Merivale had intercepted him that morning but she was now under the impression that Mr. Frensham had left Town on the north bound Mail.

At the same hour that Simon returned to Clifford Street, a querulous Mr. Cuffe was climbing back into the Bath to London coach at Hounslow, after an indigestibly short stop for refreshment; and the Hon. John Frensham, having taken the reins impatiently from his coachman, was flying along the Great North Road towards Branthorpe at a cracking pace, which boded no good for the chaise whose unpaid bill had so dismayed his mother just a week before.

SIX

DURING THE week which had passed since Miss Dorville had invited Lady Amelia to ride with her, the two girls had become firm friends.

Ann had spent one afternoon at Branthorpe Park; Amelia had wanted some help in sorting through all the dresses, hats and gloves, and myriad accessories which had accumulated before her sudden departure from home nearly four years ago. Her room and possessions had evidently been left severely alone in her absence, and since her return she had not felt able to face the task of going through them. But now, with the stimulus of the forthcoming party at the Grange, she had begged Ann's assistance in the ruthless disposal of her outmoded finery.

It was nearing six o'clock and Ann was helping clear up the chaos which they had created in the bedchamber when Amelia raised her head abruptly. "There's a carriage coming down the drive!"

"Yes, and in a great hurry too, by the sound of it," commented Ann.

With a smile of realisation, Amelia said: "Oh, it must be John! He always drives like a bedlamite." She giggled. "I'm sure Mr. Cuffe cannot have survived if they have kept that pace all the way from London! I must see if his face is green when he comes in."

Amelia went out quietly to the gallery which overlooked the entrance hall. Almost at once Ann heard the great studded door slam, and John Frensham's voice echoed through the rafters.

"Anybody home?" Then presumably seeing his sister, he demanded in a brusque voice: "Where's mama? And even Stagg seems to be missing."

The bedchamber door had been left open by Amelia, but Ann thought she should stay where she was unless Amelia revealed her presence to John, who certainly sounded rather agitated. She continued with the task of setting the bedchamber to rights.

"John, whatever's wrong? Where's Mr. Cuffe?" she heard Amelia ask.

"Oh, he'll be coming on later—probably tomorrow, or the day after," he told his sister impatiently.

"John! Is all this hubbub necessary? What will Mr. Cuffe think of us?" demanded the Dowager's voice suddenly. "Where *is* Cuffe?"

Ann went to the door of the bedchamber to close it, thinking she should not eavesdrop on the family conference which seemed to be developing in the hall downstairs. John's next words, however, quite removed this worthy intention from her mind.

"I have not brought Cuffe. I came back immediately because I have seen Simon in London, ma'am!"

There was a tense silence, broken eventually by the Dowager's calm voice. "I do not believe you John, you must have been foxed!"

"I was not foxed!" protested her son violently. "I have not the smallest doubt it was he."

There was another slight pause. "Did you speak with him?" his mother asked.

"No! Nor would I!" John declared in withering tones. "Such a picture of dissipation and ramshackle behaviour, you have never seen! Loitering outside a third-rate hotel with a red-headed light skirt hanging on his arm. He looked forty at least, and his clothes—"

"John, your wits appear to have gone a-begging! And your manners too! I have never heard such fustian nonsense!" the Dowager said, in crushing accents. "If you have anything further to say you had best come into the drawing-room, instead of crying it through the house like a common newspaper vendor. *Your* appearance is little short of ramshackle at the moment, I may say, and you stand in poor case to criticise. However, as you are clearly overwrought, I will not insist upon your changing before speaking to me."

Evidently stung by these strictures, he retorted: "It is scarcely to be wondered at if I am dishevilled! I have been travelling non-stop these two days!"

Ann guiltily closed the door of the bedchamber at this point. She had not heard Amelia's voice once during this dramatic exchange and guessed she must have been very shocked by the disclosures. It had become plain to Ann in their short acquaintance that her elder brother was still held high in Amelia's affections, whatever misdeeds he had been guilty of in the past.

Amelia did not return immediately to the bedchamber so Ann abstractedly started to fold up tissue paper, her mind full of the implications of John's news. Would his brother come back here now, and claim his inheritance, whatever that was? But everything must still surely depend on the Will? Thank heavens the attorney is coming soon, she thought. As to the Will, she no longer knew what to hope for, except that John should be satisfied with whatever fell to him, and she suspected there was small chance of that unless he had a lion's share of everything. Her mother, she knew, was anxious that their betrothal should be announced on her birthday, but Ann had been hoping for a delay. She was conscious of a growing feeling that she would not be sorry if the return of John's brother in some way prevented their marriage, but she could not suppose this was likely.

Only a few minutes had elapsed when Amelia returned. "I'm so sorry Ann, to abandon you in this ill-mannered fashion. I have sent to the stables for your horse, and a groom will see you home."

The gay intimacy of the afternoon had vanished, and she realised her friend was simply being the dutiful hostess now. "Thank you, but there was no call to turn out one of your men for a half mile ride, even in the dark."

Lady Amelia looked vaguely at the clock. "I do hope you will not be too late for dinner," she said politely.

Ann also saw the time and was astonished it was still barely six o'clock. "Oh no, a few minutes will not signify."

The two girls walked side by side down the broad stairway in silence, but when Ann had her riding coat on and was picking up her whip and gloves, she felt she had to refer to John's arrival before she left. "Convey my regards to Mr. Frensham if you will, and I hope he is not too fatigued after his journey."

"Of course I will! Forgive me if I seem a little distracted—John's sudden arrival has thrown us all into a confusion. The servants too it seems, for there is no one to open the door." She looked about her. "Ah, here's Stagg," she said with relief, as the butler approached with his customary even tread, and seeming far from confused.

As Ann took her leave she guessed her friend was

anxious to question her brother about his astonishing news; and in this surmise she was correct.

As soon as the door closed, Amelia turned and, pulling her favourite cashmere shawl closely about her, hurried to the drawing-room. Although the shawl, a rich scarlet, could scarcely be termed compatible with mourning, she had recently taken to wearing it about the house because it was the only gift she had ever received from Simon while he was in India. The Dowager had been pleased to countenance this minor transgression as it relieved the air of gloom about her daughter and flattered her fair colouring; she had, at the same time, discouraged Amelia's intention of wearing a cap indoors—a dowdy habit which the Dowager considered the outside of enough in one so young.

When Amelia joined her mother and brother, John was standing sullenly, hands behind his back, looking dwarfed beneath the huge carved stone overmantel; and the Dowager, seated on his right, was staring into the fire.

She acknowledged Amelia's arrival with a brief smile. "Your brother has a curious tale to relate, my dear, and I do not scruple to say that I am far from convinced of its truth."

Amelia looked up at John, from her chair facing her mother. "When was it you thought you saw him?" she asked.

John scowled. "I do not *think* I saw him—I did! It was the night before last," he continued wearily, "sometime between five and six I suppose. A friend was driving me home from Duke Street in his phaeton."

"It must have been quite a dark night then?" suggested his sister.

"Dark it may have been, but he was standing in the full glare of the hotel lights and I was not distracted at the time by driving or anything else. I can still see the deplorable picture he presented quite clearly in my mind. However, none of that is to the purpose," he said, starting to pace the carpet. "The proof was in the hotel book when I sent Lydd round there first thing the next morning."

Amelia looked dismayed at this, but the Dowager interposed: "Very indiscreet that was too! Doubtless the whole of Sackville Street knows by now that enquiries were made after Branthorpe as if he were a common criminal."

John checked his pacing and, with an air of exaggerated patience, explained. "Lydd had not the least idea it was my brother he was asking about. I told him a Banbury tale about a long lost cousin called Frensham whom I thought may be staying at the hotel."

"Nonetheless, I am persuaded that the butler would think it odd in you that you did not enquire for yourself," the Dowager persisted.

"Of course he did not ma'am! And how could I risk coming face to face with my brother after all these years in an hotel? You would have preferred it had I sent Joliffe, I collect?" he concluded in tones of bitter sarcasm.

Amelia thought her mother was being a bit unfair with John, but hazarded that she did not want to believe his tale and was seeking to discredit him in any way she could.

"But what proof *did* you find there?" Amelia asked him.

"Well, there was no Frensham recorded, but Lydd ascertained that a Mr. French had stayed the previous night there—A Simon French. So it's pretty conclusive, isn't it?" he appealed to them. "The state he was in, he *would* be using a spurious name—and thank heaven for it, I say."

"John, I forbid you to speak to your elder brother in that way! On your own admittance this man looked forty and can, therefore, have borne little resemblance to Simon when *you* last saw him. The name French is clearly just a coincidence," the Dowager asserted to her son's obvious disgust.

"He was with a woman, you said?" pursued Amelia.

"Yes, he was," affirmed John briefly, "but I think it wiser if I say nothing further on the subject. With your permission, ma'am, I will go and freshen up after the journey."

He strode from the room leaving the two ladies thoughtful.

"Do you really not believe him, mama?" Amelia asked, half-hoping that Simon was in England, whatever the circumstances.

"How could it be true? If he has been here for any length of time at all, he would have been recognised by more than your brother—his was a well-known face in Town. He would also be bound to know of his father's death by this time, surely? And he may be stubborn but I cannot feel he would prolong his exile in that event. He *knows* you were welcomed back here, and I suggested to him that *he* might be, even before Branthorpe died."

"But mama, if Simon left India months ago he would not have received your letters—or mine," Amelia interjected.

The Dowager considered this objection. "Perhaps you are right, but I still do not believe he would have returned to live in London of all places—and under a false name! It is not in character. Neither is the redhead, I may say!" she stated sardonically. "Nor any of the accusations of dissolute living with which his brother saw fit to charge him."

Amelia twisted her locket about as she always did

when she was worried. "No," she said at last, "I think you are right. I cannot imagine Simon behaving in such a manner. Why, he was so nice in his dress, and even without Joliffe, I do not think he would allow himself to sink so low."

The Dowager gave a surprising chuckle. "That great-coat John described would have given Joliffe a decided spasm, I warrant! But no," she reiterated firmly, "I do not believe one word of it, and I think we would do well to disregard the whole tale."

"Well, even if it *were* true, he clearly has no intention of ever coming back to us," Amelia said sadly.

The Dowager looked sharply at her daughter. "I wish you will not refine so on the matter and think yourself into a fit of the dismals! I am persuaded John's tantrums will be quite enough for me to bear in the coming days. I must place my trust in Cuffe, I suppose. His arrival does seem to be imminent at last, although I could wish John had waited and brought him in the chaise. He will be in poor case if he has to travel on the York Mail after a dose of the influenza."

*   *   *

For the second time in the space of fifteen minutes, Mr. Dorville drew out his watch, frowned at it, sighed and went on reading his paper.

His wife, who had left shortly before without saying a word, came back into the room and said complacently: "There, I've put the dinner back an hour."

Mr. Dorville looked at her over his reading glasses in open-mouthed astonishment. "An hour! Good Lord, what ever for?" He was genuinely taken aback by this unexpected announcement. If Ann was but a minute overdue in her return home, it was usually sufficient to throw his wife into a quake speculating on the various causes for the delay, but even so she had never upset their routine in this cavalier fashion. On this occasion, she had said not one word about her daughter's continued absence, but had deprived him casually of his dinner.

"I wanted to give Ann plenty of time to get home, that's all," she said in a voice of sweet reason, to which he was quite unaccustomed.

"But dammit, she's only up at the Park—she'll be here any minute, I'll be bound," muttered her husband, impatiently rustling the pages of his newspaper in an endeavour to find some item he had not read twice-over already.

"I think it is likely she may have been unavoidably delayed," explained Mrs. Dorville serenely. Her sharp ears had in fact heard the chaise hurtle past the Grange a short while before, and on such an unfrequented road as theirs this could only mean one thing: it was on its way to Branthorpe Park and must contain Mr. Frensham and Mr. Cuffe. What a fortunate thing Ann was there, she thought gleefully, she would bring home first hand news of the travellers.

She could scarcely settle to her needlework, and indeed had little opportunity to do so for horses' hooves were presently heard outside.

"There," said her husband in a disgruntled fashion, not quite daring to add, I told you so; while his wife looked disappointed for some unfathomable reason. *Women*! he thought moodily, and not for the first time, as he was always outnumbered two to one by them.

Quite soon Ann put her head round the door and said apprehensively: "I'm sorry I am late mama, but it will take me no time at all to change. I'll be down to dinner directly."

To her surprise her mother beamed at her. "Now

don't you go worrying about changing, my love, do you come in here and talk to us."

It was Ann's turn to be no less baffled than her father; riding boots on the Aubusson carpet had never been countenanced before! Thinking she must have misheard, she reiterated: "It really won't take me a moment," and disappeared upstairs.

Mrs. Dorville made an exasperated noise, and her husband wondered vaguely what was brewing and continued to read his paper as unobtrusively as possible. Meanwhile his wife spent her time trying to thread a needle but found it difficult and crossly abandoned the attempt, pushed aside her work box, patted her beautifully coiffeured dark curls, then sighed and sat back with the air of one who was much tried.

Ann returned, in fact, in a very short time.

"Well now," said Mrs. Dorville before her daughter had had time to close the door, "and did you have a nice time at the Park, my love?" she asked in an arch manner.

During her ride home with the taciturn groom, Ann had had time to consider the events at the Park and had quickly decided not to tell her family what she had overheard there.

"Oh yes thank you mama, we had great fun! It was nice to see Lady Amelia so gay."

Mrs. Dorville was not concerned with Amelia's gaiety but before she had time to probe further, Ann spoke again.

"Have there been any more replies this afternoon to our invitations?" she asked; her birthday was just over a week away now, and the thick gilt-edged cards were already out.

"No, but we did have four acceptances with gratifying promptitude, and one of them from the Lamberts—of Kerswell, you know," she added for the enlightenment of her husband, who was not listening. "Sir William declines—gout I believe—but Lady Lambert is bringing her son Ralph and the girl, I forget her name. Such charming people," declared Mrs. Dorville, to whom the possession of a title bestowed certain charm on any holder.

"Melanie," supplied Ann. "Yes, they are a handsome family indeed, and will be an adornment to the gathering. Ralph looks prodigiously romantic with his dark curls and that poetic flowing cravat he affects," she said mischievously.

Her mother was not notable for her sense of humour. "Now Ann, I will not countenance your casting lures in that young man's direction—although it would not be an impossible match, I suppose," she said thoughtfully, before going on: "You know I have quite made up my mind that your betrothal to John Frensham should be announced sometime during the entertainment."

Her daughter was still smiling at the unlikely idea of ensnaring the aesthetic Ralph Lambert, but Mr. Dorville, who always found it advisable to listen when the words Frensham or Branthorpe were on his wife's lips, was not amused.

"I would recommend you to abandon that scheme, my dear. Matters have not advanced in that direction, nor can they until the Branthorpe estate is settled, as well you know," he told her firmly.

Ann then informed her parents that John had returned late that afternoon.

"I thought as much," said Mrs. Dorville with satisfaction. "Well, things will start to move now, I warrant, with the attorney on the spot. You see, my dear sir, it could all be settled in no time at all."

Mr. Dorville was about to reply when Ann said:

"Mr. Frensham was alone, I think, although I did not see him."

"Did not see him? How was that? I was persuaded you must have talked with him," Mrs. Dorville said, thoroughly frustrated.

Ann smiled. "It is rather a large house, mama, and I am sure he was too weary to meet visitors."

"Visitors!" cried her mother. "Why you are practically one of the family."

Mr. Dorville, wisely letting this remark and its implications pass, turned to his daughter. "No attorney still, eh?" he said, taking off his glasses.

"No, I think not, but the betrothal announcement must wait awhile yet," Ann said placatingly. "It is still too soon after the bereavement."

"True, true," agreed her father, rubbing his chin thoughtfully with his folded spectacles.

"I am persuaded the Dowager would raise no objection," asserted Mrs. Dorville. "After all she was most sanguine about your birthday celebrations."

A compromise had been reached finally between mother and daughter on the form the celebrations should take; a private dinner was to be followed by a dance, both to be accommodated quite comfortably in their own double drawing-room, which was of immense proportions. In the event, Mrs. Dorville had needed little persuasion that a small private affair in her own impressive establishment was preferable to hiring a hall at York—the nearest town of significant size—for a large formal ball. She had feared that a combination of possible bad weather, a dark night and the extra distance from home, would have given her haughtier neighbours the excuse for declining the York invitation.

Ann took the opportunity of guiding the conversation back to less vexed matters by the revelation of an item of news she had reserved specially for such a moment. "That puts me in mind of the generous offer Lady Branthorpe made to me this afternoon," Ann said, and saw her mother lean forward eagerly. "She has placed the services of their French chef, Jules, at your disposal to supervise the dinner arrangements, if you so wish."

Mrs. Dorville flushed with pleasure and raised her hands. "Well, I do call that kind! How shall I ever thank her? Is not that most liberal in her ladyship, my dear?" she appealed to her husband.

"Oh yes, indeed," replied Mr. Dorville dejectedly, seeing the prospect of a good solid, edible dinner—the only aspect of the entertainment he relished—being snatched away from him in return for insubstantial foreign stuff which would doubtless run up vast bills.

His wife turned to Ann. "Now whyever did you not mention this before when you came in? There is such a lot we must discuss." With a sudden intake of breath, she said: "Oh, I have just had the most dresdful thought! Does Jules speak English do you think?"

Ann laughed. "I think he must you know, I cannot imagine he has a very comfortable time at Branthorpe if he does not. He has been there for years, in fact I believe it was the eldest son who instated him before he left. However, do not put yourself about on that head, I will interpret for you if necessary."

"Oh, of course you can my love, I quite forgot! It will be nice for you to put your expensive education to some purpose, I dare say," she said condescendingly.

Ann knew her mother regarded any kind of learning as unnecessary in a woman, but nevertheless she winced slightly at the tone of the remark.

For the next few minutes the ladies' discussion ranged widely over side dishes and removes, fish and fowl in season, jellies and sweetmeats, until Mr. Dorville was constrained to say, in strangled accents: "If you will not serve dinner in this house, at least I beg you will not talk constantly of food!"

With affronted dignity Mrs. Dorville went to the bellpull, and Ann could not help betraying a momentary flicker of amusement when her father rolled his eyes ceilingwards in a theatrical manner.

SEVEN

Josiah Cuffe did not present a very heartening sight to the assembled company. Seated behind his late client's desk in the book-room at Branthorpe Park he looked conspicuously out of place. He wore a bag wig and his dress was outmoded, which was common enough in elderly attorneys, but he also had a considerable length of flannel wound about his throat, almost reaching his ears, and giving the impression of a grubby but exceedingly fashionable high collar. Mr. Cuffe's plain, rather flat features were illuminated on this occasion by a grog-blossom nose, due to the combined effects of influenza, and its subsequent spirituous treatment and prolonged exposure in cold coaches. None of this served to diminish in any way, however, the rapt attention of his audience. The Dowager

Countess of Branthorpe, her daughter and youngest son, together with the steward, whom no one had dared exclude, all listened silently to the attorney's somewhat hoarse rendering of the long-awaited contents of the Will, which Mr. Cuffe had brought with him late that morning. He had arrived in a parlous state, but his revival had been quite marked after a well-timed nuncheon.

As soon as the words "signed this thirtieth day of November in the year of our Lord eighteen hundred and twelve," the Dowager spoke to forestall John launching into a flood of questions, which were obviously imminent. "Mr. Cuffe let me say at once how sorry I am that you have been compelled to perform this onerous task when you should quite clearly keep to your bed. However, I am sure you understand that as this was such a recent and unexpected Will you must bear with a few of our questions. It is, I collect, quite valid?"

Mr. Cuffe ceased dabbing at his long-suffering nose and hastily put away a snuff-stained handkerchief. "Oh indeed yes, there is no possible doubt," he croaked, and nodded.

"Then—correct me if I mistake the matter—my eldest son Simon is sole legatee of the bulk of the estate and his father's fortune. Amelia is to have the benefit of £500 a year, and I have my jointure of course. The Wragston estate is to fall to John," and here she glanced at her son, who was maintaining a brooding silence throughout this exchange, "together with the income therefrom, as we expected, but there is now no provision for additional income when he marries. Am I right?"

"Just so. It was an unfortunate circumstance, putting it at its mildest, that his lordship should have signed the new Will before the Marriage Settlement. He had every intention, as I am sure you are aware, of settling a considerable income on Mr. Frensham on his forthcoming marriage, and as this was imminent when he signed the new Will it was left out of the depositions. Meaning, of course, that Mr. Frensham has now forfeited that income. Most unfortunate," he reiterated, and wagged his head solemnly.

"It's monstrous!" John fulminated. "We all know that that money was intended for me. Why should I not have it? My elder brother is not even here to take his share—or his responsibilities either," he said bitterly.

Mr. Cuffe sniffed. "Er, yes, it is particularly regrettable in the circumstances that the heir himself should be absent. For if he were so disposed, the Settlement could still be made—although I hasten to add this would be entirely a matter for his discretion." His nose seemed to attain new heights of rosiness with embarrassment.

"Well, he *is* absent, so what's to be done?" asked John irascibly. "Our affairs cannot be at a stand for ever because of him."

Mr. Cuffe fought on valiantly. "Matters need not languish. Although the principal cannot be touched, the estate can still be run—the late Earl gave his widow the power of attorney. And the Wragston estate is, I fancy, a considerable one and lies entirely at your disposal, Mr. Frensham," the attorney pointed out with no great optimism.

Featherstone, the steward, interposed here, with unusual temerity. "It is indeed, and, if I may venture to suggest, it could raise far greater revenues with some skilful management which has been so lacking in recent years."

If all this was meant to placate Mr. Frensham it did

not succeed in its purpose. "But is Mr. Dorville going to look kindly on my suit now? Tell me that?"

Mr. Cuffe cleared his throat noisily. "Clearly, I cannot speak for him, but I would not have supposed it out of the question that he should do so. He is a man of some financial understanding and has an appreciation, I dare swear, of a fortune dependent on the land rather than the whims of the stock market and banks—particularly in these uncertain times. However," he put in quickly, "it is not for me to say, although I am willing to do all I can to further your interests of course."

This time his words did seem to have given John pause for thought. "It may be possible, I suppose, to wrest sufficient funds from the Wragston estate to support a few hunters and a couple of carriages," he said presently, as one prepared to indulge in the ultimate in retrenchment.

Mr. Cuffe eyed him warily. "The stables and stock here are deemed to be part of the Branthorpe estate, you understand," he explained with evident apprehension.

"What!" cried John, aghast. "All the hunters and our string of racehorses? Surely not?"

Featherstone intervened rashly again. "You will no doubt discover Mr. Cuffe, that some of their number are not even paid for as yet," he suggested, only to be rewarded by a black look from the attorney.

"And some of them are!" retorted John in savage tones. "Why a few are worth £700 and more apiece. Am I to keep none of them?"

"Your own saddle horse would not be included," wheezed Mr. Cuffe, bent on disaster.

"Saddle horse be damned!" roared Mr. Frensham in a surprisingly resonant voice for one of slight build, and he strode out slamming the door behind him.

"Disregard him, Mr. Cuffe, I beg you," said the Dowager calmly. "He will come about in time, but I fear he has been a spoiled child these many years. I am persuaded that if he has Wragston to set to rights and a sensible wife to help him, it will be the making of him. I hope you may be right about Dorville," she added.

"Yes, let us hope so," the attorney agreed absently, an uncertain expression on his raw face. "There is another small matter I think I should bring to your notice, m'lady, if I could have a private word in your ear," he proposed in troubled accents.

The Dowager dismissed the steward with the promise that Cuffe would be at his service shortly; and Amelia, who had said not one word throughout the fraught proceedings, took leave of her mother, and left her with the attorney.

"Now Cuffe, what skeleton have you laid bare in the family cupboard?" she asked brusquely.

He seemed unnerved by the choice of phrase and blinked his watering eyes in her direction. "I scarcely know how to broach such a delicate matter—"

"Come now, Cuffe, if it is a question of supporting some by-blow of my late husband, or even several, you need have no qualms. I shall throw you no spasms," her ladyship said prosaically.

"Good God no! Nothing of that nature, I assure you," exclaimed Mr. Cuffe, his forensic manner deserting him.

"You surprise me," the Dowager said mildly. "But please go on, I beg you," she urged.

"I—it may be nothing at all—in fact I'm sure it isn't, but I feel it should be brought to your ladyship's notice."

"Yes, yes," said the Dowager, impatient of these ditherings.

"Well, when I called at my Chambers a couple of days ago on arriving from Somerset, my clerk, a dim lad in all conscience, told me of a strange visitor he had had that day. Someone who called himself Wragston, Viscount Wragston. The name meant nothing to my clerk, you understand, but this stranger evidently wished to see me." He watched the Dowager closely but she betrayed no emotion. "Now, from the description the lad gave me I would say it is a hoax, yes, definitely a hoax," he repeated decisively.

"And what description was that?" her ladyship asked.

He seemed puzzled by her calm, almost disinterested reaction but was relieved she was not taking it too seriously. "Oh, a tall middle-aged gentleman, although gentleman is pitching it too strong if the clerk is to be believed! He had long dishevelled hair, and a somewhat wild and eccentric demeanour altogether, I collect. Not bearing the smallest resemblance to your eldest son," he assured her. "He gave no evidence of his identity, I may say, although was about to produce a card then seemed to think better of it, I am told. It appears to me he was obviously some impostor—possibly thinking to claim the Branthorpe inheritance, and will no doubt have second thoughts after his discouraging reception." The attorney gave a snuffling laugh.

"It would seem very unlikely, Mr. Cuffe," the Dowager said ambiguously. "But I am greatly obliged to you for telling me this, you acted quite correctly. How was it left with the visitor, should he return in your absence?"

"I should think it most improbable he would return, m'lady," he opined. "Although he did threaten to do so the next morning, so I instructed the clerk to lock the door. I had to leave early that day to come here, of course, so there was no question of my seeing him."

"Did your clerk mention to the visitor that you were travelling to Branthorpe?" her Ladyship asked.

"Oh no, certainly not. I own he is not the brightest of lads but he would not discuss my business with a stranger, I warrant. No, I'm sure he would not," he added as if to convince himself.

Seeing his worried countenance, the Dowager said reassuringly: "It does not signify, Mr. Cuffe. If this stranger is resolved in his masquerade we shall doubtless be seeing him here in due course."

Mr. Cuffe looked horrified. "I trust not, m'lady, he sounded a most undesirable character."

"I adjure you not to mention this to another soul," she warned him. "And now I will let you return to your many problems. You will find Featherstone anxiously awaiting you, I don't doubt," the Dowager said with a kindly smile, as he gathered up his papers.

She was unquestionably disturbed by Cuffe's report, and sat for a long time in the book-room considering it, together with John's tale which no longer seemed so incredible. Not without misgiving, she concluded that it must indeed be Simon who was abroad in London. That he had suffered grievously in some manner during his absence seemed proven by his ageing and unkempt appearance. The latter aspect almost persuaded her it could not be her son, for the picture she had carried in her mind since his departure was of a young man of the utmost particularity in his dress and bearing. However, she had had distressing evidence in Amelia, of what a change could be wrought in a person's physical aspect by crushing misfortune. But Simon, she was sure, had a strength of character which was lacking, so far, in his younger brother and to a lesser degree in Amelia, although the Dowager considered she had matured amazingly as a result of her trials.

If Simon was back in England again and in dire

straits, she hazarded that eventually he would make some attempt to contact his family. She had, even at the time, forgiven his youthful fatuity in helping Amelia run away, but his subsequent wrongheadedness in leaving the country had taken longer to pardon. That was all past now, and she was certainly ready to see him reinstated at Branthorpe; but undoubtedly John was not. It was essential therefore she should see John, apologise for her earlier disbelief in his story, and convince him that Simon's return was to be welcomed. Not an easy task, to be sure, but perhaps if she could persuade him that Simon would rectify the financial wrongs he had suffered he would be more favourably disposed to receive him.

She rang for the butler, whose stately form materialised in due course.

"Stagg, have Mr. Frensham sent in to me right away, would you?" she requested.

"I think your ladyship will find he is not within. He was bound for the stables some little while ago, and I would hazard he has quit the park by this time."

"Wretched boy!" declared her ladyship.

"Yes, m'lady," intoned Stagg mechanically, and withdrew.

* * *

The wretched boy was at that moment leading his horse round the magnificent stuccoed facade of Mr. Dorville's establishment towards the stables. The gardener's son, who performed all manner of duties about the stables and garden, informed him that Mr. Dorville would be discovered in one of his succession houses, it being his father's day off.

John found him in the second house, where he appeared to have created sufficient chaos in repotting some delicate seedlings to give any self-respecting gardener a fit of the apoplexy. He was enjoying himself hugely and beamed when he saw young Mr. Frensham.

"Come in, come in, my dear fellow," he said waving a trowel, and addressing his neighbour with unusual familiarity due to the informal surroundings.

John, in an agitated state, was glad of this and hoped it augured well for his mission which was not an easy one. "I wouldn't want to disturb you, but hoped I could have a quiet word," he said, in a diffident manner which would have surprised his family.

"Certainly," responded Mr. Dorville expansively. "What better place, eh? Away from the ladies, God bless 'em, and quite hidden by the misted glass! Sit down," he invited, indicating an upturned barrel.

Mr. Frensham declined, heedful of his cream buckskin breeches, but Mr. Dorville, who had no such misgivings, settled himself on a handy ledge and waited for Mr. Frensham to speak.

"Well sir, I thought you should know at once of my expectations under my father's Will."

"Ah," said Mr. Dorville comprehensively.

"I fear they are not as substantial as I had hoped— indeed had every reason to expect," he interposed with a touch of bitterness which, recollecting his audience, he quelled instantly. "In the circumstances, of course, it is only to be expected that you will look less favourably upon me as a prospective son-in-law," he said in depressed tones.

Mr. Dorville had a liking for young Mr. Frensham, regarding him as cheerful, easy-going and not possessed of overpowering bookish accomplishments which he would have found altogether too daunting combined with such superior social standing. He was sorry therefore, to hear these tidings. "Let's not prejudge the matter," he said cautiously. "I hope I am not an unreasonable man."

John then explained about the Wragston estate, putting forth extensive and necessarily extemporary schemes for its improvement as he had hitherto not taken the smallest interest in the property. He presented an altogether wholesome picture of thrift and husbandry in which nothing less sturdy than a shire horse could possibly have figured; hunters and race horses might never have existed for him.

Mr. Dorville listened, a trifle surprised by this earnest exposition of estate management, but told himself that after all he did not know Mr. Frensham very well; neither was his knowledge of agriculture very extensive, fortunately for John. The loss of income due to Mr. Frensham on his marriage was a great pity, but he had to own that his presentation of the potential Wragston finances compensated for this in some degree.

"Well, Mr. Frensham, I appreciate your frankness in this matter. Never did like doing business by a side wind! I'll get in touch with my attorney and we'll let him thrash it out with your man, eh?" he said bluffly.

John expressed his thanks for Mr. Dorville's generosity, then added humbly: "It is, if I may say so sir, rather more than a business arrangement to me." He looked a little uncomfortable, a slight flush rising to the fair hair brushed forward about his temples. "You may not be aware that I hold your daughter very high in my affections. Ann is very dear to me and it would be a blow of the utmost severity were the marriage to be prevented at this stage," he confessed earnestly.

Mr. Dorville had indeed been in ignorance of Mr. Frensham's feelings and this fervent declaration was a complete surprise to him. "I see, I see," he murmured, disconcerted.

There was a brief uneasy silence, then John said

briskly: "Thank you for hearing me out, sir. I am most indebted to you."

Mr. Dorville, recalled to his duties as host by this speech, asked Mr. Frensham to come indoors where the ladies would doubtless be delighted to offer him some refreshment.

The young man politely declined the invitation, and Mr. Dorville escorted him to the stables, then returned to the succession house, where he sank thoughtfully on to the barrel. It seemed odd in Mr. Frensham after his protestations to reject an opportunity to see his love, he thought, but perhaps he wished matters to be settled before he spoke with her again. Mr. Dorville could not but be pleased by his future son-in-law's sentiments and he hoped the financial arrangements were going to be satisfactory; crying off would certainly present more difficulties now.

When Ann came in search of her father some time later, she found him still seated on the keg, looking for all the world like a large corpulent gnome, she thought.

"Mama thought she heard a visitor," she said.

"And she sent you to investigate, eh? Well there was—Mr. Frensham looked in to tell me that their attorney has arrived and matters can go forward again."

"He knows what his expectations are then?" Ann asked, slight apprehension in her voice.

"Yes, kitten, he does," her father said gently, "and although he has suffered a disappointment in respect of his income, he has taken it remarkably well. I was quite impressed by his good sense I may say. I think you may take it all will be well now with the Settlement."

The removal of the uncertainty surrounding her future was a relief in itself, and she received the news with equanimity if no demonstrable joy. Her father knew she was not given to excessive displays of emotion, having a very equable temperament, and was not surprised when she simply smiled and said: "I am pleased to hear that. Mr. Frensham must be vastly relieved too."

He was not convinced that relief had been one of Mr. Frensham's emotions that afternoon but forebore to say so. He also decided to keep his counsel in regard to Mr. Frensham's declaration of love for Ann; he had no notion whether his daughter was acquainted with her future husband's feelings for her but was quite sure that young man was capable of informing her himself.

"It does appear now that your betrothal will be certain by your birthday, but I think we will have no public announcements about it until the three months' mourning period is over," he warned her as they walked back to the house.

Ann was quite happy to agree to this, and also to the suggestion that she accompany her father to York the following Monday.

"I wish to see my attorney, and I am persuaded you have plenty of commissions to carry out there for your forthcoming dance."

"Oh yes, indeed! My ball dress should be ready by then."

It was not to be expected that Mrs. Dorville would greet the news of Mr. Frensham's reduced prospects with approbation. However, in due course she came to agree with her husband that he was still an eligible *parti* for their daughter. She was less tractable when it came to persuading her that the young gentleman's affections were engaged. Later that day when Ann had retired for the night, Mr. Dorville gave his wife an account of what John Frensham had told him.

"Fiddlesticks!" his spouse declared. "He has concealed it most admirably in that event, but I'll have none of it! Nor will Ann I warrant."

Mr. Dorville was alarmed. "I wish you will not mention it to Ann, my dear. We should permit the young people to resolve their feelings in their own way."

"My dear sir, I have not the smallest need to refer to my daughter on this head," she said, affronted. "It is as plain as the way to the parish church that this is no love match—but it's none the worse for that," she stated in forthright accents.

* * *

It soon became apparent that Mr. Dorville had been mistaken in thinking that John was avoiding Ann. She was engaged to ride with Lady Amelia the following afternoon and as she waited at the gates of Shipton Grange she was surprised to see both Mr. Frensham and his sister riding towards her.

She felt a little embarrassed by the unexpected meeting as she had not spoken with him since his return from London. But, on reflection she decided that from the little she knew of him, it was tolerably certain the conversation would quickly centre round equine matters rather than anything of a personal nature. He greeted her very warmly, but then rode behind the two girls as they made their way through the quiet hamlet of Branthorpe.

The sky was clear and the air sharp, and there had been no snow as yet. "It will be most fortunate for your party if this weather holds for another sennight," Amelia said to her friend, and for the next few minutes the talk was of Ann's birthday celebrations, now exactly a week away.

But when they were about a mile past Branthorpe Amelia turned abruptly to Ann and said: "You will not mind if I leave you in John's care for a while will you? There is a call I promised to make nearby," she explained vaguely. "I will not be long away, and will rejoin you again at the cross-roads."

Ann deduced that this was a pre-arrangement between brother and sister, for Amelia merely called over her shoulder: "I am going now John, and will be back in half an hour."

"Very well," he returned, an edge of disapproval in his voice. "But be careful!"

"I will," his sister promised, with a sudden blithe smile, which took Ann by surprise. Puzzled, she watched the black-cloaked figure canter ahead of them. Amelia was quickly forgotten though when she realised she was alone with her future husband for the first time. She had been acquainted with John Frensham for almost two years but their meetings had been largely at formal gatherings in the district, or at Meets; and since plans for their marriage had been broached, just before the Earl's death, they had seen even less of each other.

John drew his horse level with hers, but made no attempt to move off. "I hope you will forgive my little stratagem," he said, smiling. "I wanted to see you alone."

"I am persuaded my reputation will survive," she responded cheerfully. "We are unlikely to be overlooked by any gossip-mongers on this quiet stretch of road."

"You are not forgetting either, I trust, that we are practically betrothed?" He raised his fair brows and darted an anxious glance at her. "Your father told you of my visit yesterday, I collect, Miss Dorville? Dash it! I may call you Ann, mayn't I?" he added impatiently.

She laughed. "Yes, to both questions, Mr. Frensham."

"You had best make it John henceforward," he recommended.

"I will try," she promised shyly, "but it may take me a little time to get used to it."

"You are pleased about—everything?" he asked tentatively.

Noticing the anxious furrows marring his youthful features, she reflected that although they were practically of an age, he seemed much younger than she. "Yes, of course I am," she said, as much to reassure herself as him. "And I am so glad you are to have Wragston," she went on conversationally, thinking to hear, at any moment, of his schemes for the stables there. But she was wrong.

He gave a curious, shaky laugh. "I own to being quite delighted. You see, Ann, I love you very much and would have found it unbearable had our plans been overset by some trifling financial snag."

Ann was so astonished by this outpouring she thought she must have misheard: but then he leaned towards her and placed a gloved hand on hers. "You must believe me!" he said in overwrought accents. She felt his gaze on her but was unable to meet it; at last she found her voice.

"But I had no idea—why we hardly know each other," she said in a stupefied way.

"And what has that to say to it?" he responded, slightly indignant. "I knew from the moment I saw you."

Ann managed to smile at him. "Forgive me, I am behaving rather foolishly, but—well, you must know, I do not return your sentiments I'm afraid," she told him, uncomfortably aware that her indulgent feelings of seniority had fled.

He released her hand. "That does not signify," he said carelessly. "I am persuaded we shall deal very well together."

"Should we not ride on? The horses will take a chill," she commented, and thought wildly that that must prove his sincerity; he had forgotten his horse's welfare!

They rode on, and presently she told him that her father was seeing his attorney the following week about the Settlement.

"Sound man, your father," John commented. "I have a great admiration for his good sense."

"It appears to be mutual! He said almost the same of you. Your schemes for Wragston impressed him enormously."

He grinned. "Oh that! Well, I hope I know something of estate management. I have had to take the reins in my brother's absence, you know," he remarked, a shade pompously Ann thought.

John had not mentioned his brother before and she knew she was on rather delicate ground. "It must have made things difficult for you," she said sympathetically.

He snorted. "They'd be more devilish difficult if he came back!"

She kept silent, recalling John's strictures on his brother overheard by her at Branthorpe.

"I hope you will like it in Lincolnshire," he said abandoning the subject of his brother, to her relief. "It's wonderful riding country near Wragston."

"I'm sure I shall," she replied, barely suppressing a smile. "What is the house like?"

"Wragston? Oh, a great rambling stone edifice—not as big as Branthorpe, thank God, but nearly as old. But marvellous stables!" he exclaimed, suddenly enthusiastic. "Brick you know, specially built. Stone is bad for horses—too damp."

"I see, but it is good enough for us, I suppose?" she retorted ironically.

However, as she had suspected, John had little sense of humour, particularly where horses were concerned. He continued to expound on his beasts' welfare, until he said suddenly: "We'd better turn back now or we shall miss Amelia."

The countryside was very flat and as they rode towards the cross-roads Ann noticed Amelia turning out of a narrow lane. So she had been to Kerswell, Ann thought, wondering what could take her there; she couldn't recollect having heard Amelia speak of the Lamberts. She tried to remember her reaction when Amelia had been told that the romantic-looking Ralph and his sister had accepted invitations to her party, but could not recall anything significant. It was quite evident, however, that the visit had had an inspiriting effect on Amelia. When she joined them for the ride home her eyes were sparkling.

"Were you seen?" Ann heard John ask his sister in an undertone.

She shook her head.

"Well, it can't go on, you know," he muttered, and Ann saw Amelia's face cloud over momentarily. But it was a brief exchange, and then John rode behind the girls again.

For the remainder of the trot home Amelia chatted easily with Ann, whose mind was now preoccupied with the various revelations concerning her two companions during the past hour.

EIGHT

THE CHAISE rattled under the archway and into the yard of the York posting-house, then with a cry from the driver, and a jingle of harness it stopped, and for a few seconds there was silence. But not for long. An ostler appeared, ready to change the horses in minutes if need be, but this service was not required as the postboys swiftly informed him. Instead the yellow door was opened, the steps pulled down and, to the ostler's gratification, a member of the Quality emerged accompanied by another fine-looking gentleman. The latter proceeded into the Swan posting-house while the former stayed in the yard conferring with the postboys and ostler, and made various disbursements. When these arrangements were concluded to the satisfaction of all concerned, Simon followed Mr. Trant inside.

Philip was already seated in the deserted coffee-room in a corner; two tankards before him. The settle-like wooden seats afforded them some measure of seclusion.

"Well, Phil, all has gone like clockwork, so far," said Simon with evident relief.

Philip thought his friend looked every inch an Earl

now, and wished his mother could have witnessed the startling metamorphosis. From the moment, five days earlier, that Simon had returned depressed from his second abortive visit to Mr. Cuffe's Chambers, and Philip had subsequently managed to persuade his friend that the most likely place to find the Lady Amelia was at Branthorpe Park, Simon had decided to return to his native Yorkshire.

"Yes, this morning's run from Sherburn took barely 90 minutes. The clock has just struck ten," Philip said, nodding at the ancient timepiece standing in the corner. "Have you despatched your messenger to Branthorpe?"

"Ay, the deed is done," his lordship sighed. "By noon or thereabouts I should have my mother's reply to hand."

Philip was not yet accustomed to the transformation in his friend, although he had been travelling with him nearly three days from London; from his high-crowned beaver hat down to the brilliant top boots, he presented a picture in the first style of elegance. His black superfine tail-coat was moulded to his lean figure in a manner which spoke volumes for the skill of his hard pressed tailor; a black starched cravat was arranged in the simple Hunting tie over the stiff snowy shirt collar as he was out of touch with the folds and intricacies required for the more fashionable elaborate neckcloth styles.

"Will it be wise to remain here all morning?" Philip asked, as a large, gaitered gentleman came noisily into the coffee-room.

"No, although no one has recognised me yet I intend to hire a private parlour, saying I want to rest after a tiring journey. But you need not stay incarcerated with me this fine morning. I would suggest you stroll about the town and see the Minster perhaps, while I ponder on my forthcoming debut at Branthorpe. If it is to be permitted, of course! I cannot rid myself of the conviction that my brother is installed there with wife and a brood of sturdy heirs."

Philip laughed. "Even so, it would take a stony-hearted mother indeed to turn away her first-born in these circumstances."

The Earl gave him a rueful look. "We seem to run to hard hearts in our family, though not on the distaff side, I grant you."

"I will bespeak the parlour in my name for you," Philip offered.

"Thank you. Phil. Lord, I'm tired to death of this charade," Simon said wearily. "I hope at least that this is the last time I need skulk in private parlours."

"I am persuaded it will be," Philip told him in rallying tones. He had been delighted when Simon asked for his company on this fateful journey, but recalling his friend's wild talk of going to the Americas to fight in the war there, if he should be turned off by his family, Philip would be glad when the outcome of their journey was known.

By the time Philip came back about noon, Simon, who had been reduced to reading out-of-date newspapers in the parlour, had had his fill of isolation and suggested they partook of a nuncheon downstairs in the dining-room. "After all," he explained, "my family must know of my presence now and I will risk an encounter with a garrulous old friend at this stage."

The dining-room of the Swan was quiet although, due to its being market day, one or two of the farming fraternity were having a bibulous repast in one corner of the room. The only other occupants were an autocratic-looking middle-aged matron and her harassed female companion; the matron had on a lead a mournful spaniel which was sitting under their table. As these ladies were quite unknown to his lordship he selected a nearby table, and one which faced the door, so that he should not be taken unawares by an acquaintance. It was then that the Vision appeared.

Philip became increasingly conscious of the fact that his words were falling on deaf ears and, turning his head slowly, he followed the direction of Simon's gaze. He looked back at his friend in alarm. "She a friend of yours?" he hissed.

"Would she were," came the surprising response.

The young lady settled herself, together with a large number of bandboxes, at a table near the door. Before reluctantly withdrawing his gaze, his lordship had taken cognizance of a very self-possessed young woman delectably clad in a dove-grey velvet pelisse, frogged, and with a bonnet and muff, all lavishly trimmed with sable.

Fortunately the waiter diverted his attention in a broad Yorkshire accent, once so familiar to him and now sounding quite alien. He plied the two gentlemen with dishes piled high with rabbit and onions, stewed pigeons and cabbage, pigs' trotters fried in batter and Yorkshire pudding, until Philip's round face glowed in appreciation of this northern bounty.

Simon, however, did small justice to his native fare having little appetite as every minute might herald the messenger's return from Branthorpe. Soon, the antics of the dog under the nearby table claimed his notice. A large, succulent piece of pie had been inadvertently dropped within the animal's ken, and his eyes were fixed mournfully upon it. His range, though, was limited by the erratic movement of his oblivious mistress's arm which held the lead. Simon watched in fascination as time and again the small jaws scooped at the pie and missed by a hair's breadth. But at last a successful lunge was made; the tit-bit disappeared in one gulp and a look of foolish complacency spread over the spaniel's face. His lordship chuckled to himself, and then discovered the entertainment had been shared. The Vision's laughing eyes met his in mutual appreciation of this minor canine triumph.

Philip, although engrossed in his victuals, did note, with some surprise, that his friend seemed to be grinning admiringly in the direction of the strange unaccompanied young female. Perhaps it was merely the Yorkshire friendliness he had heard so much about; however, when his lordship rose suddenly with a brief word of excuse and appeared to be heading in the direction of that same young lady, Philip thought it the outside of enough.

Fortunately, before any word of restraint could pass his lips, he recollected he was not responsible for his young friend's behaviour. He realised that, during the past months, he had become accustomed to ministering to Simon and was in danger of assuming the role of governor if he did not take care. There was no cause for anxiety in this instance though, as Philip discovered when he cast a sidelong glance towards the doorway. The young lady was sitting demurely on her own, quite unmolested.

Simon was in the yard talking with the horse-keeper, and consulting his fob watch. "It's barely twenty miles there and back," his lordship was saying in fretting tones. "He should be here now. I'll wager he has cast a shoe," he declared accusingly.

" 'Ere, there's nowt like that there wi' my 'osses," protested the horse-keeper, stung into the vernacular. "Ah, 'ere's t'lad now," he said, relieved that his reputation was saved by the timely arrival of the messenger.

His relief was as nought compared with that experienced by Simon when he tore open the thick, black-edged paper and read the brief message, under the familiar Branthorpe crest, in his mother's well-known fist. "Welcome home" was all it said. He had, in his own very difficult note, cautiously instructed her to use the name French in directing her reply. But beyond stating he had returned to England unexpectedly due to sickness, and had heard since of his father's death, he had only mentioned there was a good friend accompanying him. He had not been able to bring himself to ask about his sister at this stage. With a full heart he now stared at the two words as if they were a talisman—as indeed they were; he was roused ultimately by the messenger leading away his sweating bay.

Still dazed, Simon called him back, fetched out his purse and gave the rider a guinea. Gold had an ever more riveting effect in these impoverished parts than in London. The post boy remarked to his envious cronies later, whilst still fingering the guinea lovingly: "Ay, 'e were Quality right enough, nowt like them jumped-up folk from t'mills as comes 'ere chucking their weight, and nowt much else, about."

His lordship, slowly grasping the fact that nothing now stood between him and his home except a suitable conveyance, addressed the horse-keeper again requesting a chaise to carry him to Branthorpe. This gentleman had glimpsed the passage of gold to his colleague and was therefore not pleased to hear a hearty voice calling across the yard. "Branthorpe? Did I hear you say Branthorpe?"

Simon also was not pleased, fearing to recognise one of his more pushing old acquaintances.

"Forgive me for intruding but I am just this minute having the horses put to, before driving to Branthorpe myself. I'd be most honoured if you would accept a place in my carriage, sir."

His lordship turned and saw it was a broad-shouldered, ruddy-faced gentleman who addressed him and, to his vast relief, a total stranger. "I am greatly obliged to you, sir, but I am travelling with a friend and am much encumbered by luggage."

"But that's of no consequence I assure you; there will be ample room for the four of us," the stranger responded genially.

Simon did not feel in conversable mood on this of all journeys and, with great charm, he declined the kind offer. The refusal was well-taken and the gentleman withdrew, allowing the relieved horse-keeper to take full charge of the situation once more. A chaise and pair were promised to be ready within minutes and, if the reverential manner was any indication, it seemed likely to be the best equipage in the stables.

Still not quite comprehending the fact that he was almost home again, Simon went back to find his friend. Now fully embarked on a custard tart with some baked apples, Philip was exactly where his lordship had left him. He rejoined him at the table. "I trust you will feel able to travel again soon, after all this indulgence," his lordship said with a sardonic smile.

"This? But this is a mere whet—" he said, then a forkful of apple was checked in mid-air. "You've heard?" he asked wide-eyed.

"Yes, I've heard and all's well," Simon told him, momentarily overwhelmed as relief swept over him again.

"But that's capital!—I say are you feeling quite the thing?" he asked, as his lordship drew a hand across his brow. Philip had watched him, Argus-eyed, these past weeks and although he had been astonished by Simon's recovery from the fever, he still feared a possible relapse due to worry and strain.

"Yes, you old wherreter! My mother seems to have taken the news with remarkable northern stolidity if her concise reply is any guide. But I own I'll breathe more freely when the family reunion is over." He looked about him to hail the waiter for a sustaining brandy, and saw that the Vision, whom he had forgotten utterly, was in earnest converse with the florid gentleman who had offered his carriage. He recollected now that something had been said about room for four, and cursed his ill-luck at having to reject such a travelling companion.

A few minutes later the couple left the dining-room and his lordship acknowledged their departing smiles with an affable nod, promising himself he would discover the lady's name once he was settled at Branthorpe.

*   *   *

It was not to be supposed that the residents of Branthorpe Park would remain unaffected on being told of the imminent return of their lord and master, but the degree of joy expressed by individuals varied enormously. Thus the Dowager, who might be expected to be the most moved by this event, preserved a calm dignity throughout, and Jules, a mere servant, albeit an upper one of some importance, was quite overset by the news and made no secret of the tears of joy which coursed down his sallow cheeks. He had particular cause for elation as his services had gone largely unappreciated since his lordship's disappearance, and he had only stayed on in such a barbaric northern household because he nursed a *tendre* for the Dowager's maid, Ellis. The chef had spent a trying morning with Mrs. Dorville at the Grange and, when he heard the good news on his return, his Gallic temperament was already much agitated by the recent confrontation with the modern kitchen at the Grange and its new, fiendish Bodley stove.

Another inmate, also an upper servant, was much

affected by the tidings when imparted to him by the Dowager herself, but Joliffe would have considered the least sign of emotion as unseemly in a gentleman's gentleman.

Lady Amelia, when her mother gave her Simon's note to read, shed a few brief tears of relief but soon recovered her composure, and awaited her brother's arrival with great eagerness.

The Dowager, who had been half-expecting to hear from Simon, warned her daughter later that his appearance might still give some cause for alarm. "I am persuaded, from the various reports that have come to my notice, that the illness he has suffered must have been of great severity."

"But he's home mama! He will soon recover now. Jules shall prepare his favourite dinner tonight; I will go and see him about it right away," said Amelia, almost running to the drawing-room door.

"And leave me to face John, I suppose," the Dowager said grimly. "Where is the boy? The news will be all over the estate by now, and he'll not be pleased to hear it—least of all from the servants."

Amelia hesitated by the door. "I'm not sure, mama, but out shooting I fancy."

"Well off you go, my dear. He will seek me out soon enough when he does return, I'll warrant." The Dowager had approached John several days ago, on his complacent return from seeing Mr. Dorville, and put it to him that his brother should be welcomed if he did come home. John had said he wanted none of him or his money; he would soon be married to the woman he loved, (and here the Dowager had raised her eyebrows a little) and living miles away from them all at Wragston. His mother had soon relinquished the task of persuading him, and now had little hope of prevailing upon him to greet his brother with any semblance of goodwill.

The Dowager had already spent some time soothing Mr. Cuffe who, on hearing of the heir's return, was inconsolable over the treatment his lordship had received at the hands of his uncouth, incompetent clerk. However, the prospect of being able to hand over the affairs of the estate into their rightful hands and apply for probate without complications, was a great alleviation to him, and together with Featherstone, who was also much enlivened by the news, he returned to the mountain of paper-work with a new enthusiasm.

Luncheon was over now and an air of expectancy hung about the great house, but John had still not returned.

* * *

The Earl of Branthorpe leaned forward in the chaise as the squat, square tower of Branthorpe Church appeared on the horizon.

"Almost there," he murmured to Philip, but continued to watch the passing flat, familiar landscape. Presently he startled his friend by saying abruptly: "Good God, what's that?"

Philip looked out of the window but could see nothing untoward.

"That house—that blain on the landscape!" his lordship said violently; then as the carriage slowed to turn in at the main sweepgates of Branthorpe Park, he said: "Why it must be where the old Grange was! Whatever possessed them to allow that? Sorry Phil," he apologised, suddenly relaxing. "I'll have to get used to changes, I suppose."

However, there was no apparent change in his own house. As he glimpsed it between the elm trees lining the drive, he gave a nostalgic chuckle. "Look at all those Elizabethan chimneys, Phil! It was used to be a favourite game of ours as children to count them, but we never had the same number twice. I still don't know, but it's fifty or thereabouts."

"It's a magnificent place," commented Philip in awed accents.

"Yes, I suppose it is," acknowledged his lordship, seeing it with new eyes. In the past it had simply been the large, draughty edifice he lived in. "The Frenshams didn't build it. It was presented by a grateful Charles II to the first Earl who rendered him some aid."

As they approached the main entrance there was one change which he noticed with sadness; the hatchment, placed over the porch with his father's bearing and date of his death, and which would remain there for a year from that date.

Simon steeled himself for what the next few minutes might reveal, and prayed that Amelia would be there. Their arrival had been anticipated, for a footman sprang forward from the porch as the chaise stopped. Stagg, the butler, permitting himself the broadest smile in years, was the first familiar face to greet his lordship.

After instructing the footman to see that the postboys were well-entertained in the kitchen before returning to York, and having received Stagg's august welcome, Simon perceived the shadowy figure of his mother waiting just inside the great hall; she looked smaller than he remembered. As he went to greet her he saw the slim, fair figure in a red shawl beside her.

"Melly, thank God you're here!" he cried, and somehow managed to embrace both mother and sister for a brief moment.

"I vow you don't look forty," exclaimed his mother inexplicably at one point.

Condolences were offered and mutual enquiries of health satisfied. His lordship asked rather apprehensively about his brother, and was told he was expected home any moment.

Mr. Trant meanwhile, tarried with the butler prolonging the handing over of his great-coat, beaver hat, gloves and stick for as long as possible. Stagg's sense of decorum soon asserted itself however, even in this overcharged emotional atmosphere; he handed Philip's discarded raiment to a footman, saying in stentorian tones: "Bestow Mr. Trant's things in the closet."

This had the desired effect, and Simon looked round guilty. "My dear Philip, do forgive me!"

The introductions were quickly made and then after a few brief civilities the Dowager, sensing her son's great agitation, intervened. "Amelia, my dear, see that Mr. Trant is shown to his room. I will repair with your brother to the Blue Saloon."

Once there, her ladyship sat in her usual high-backed velvet chair by the side of the fireplace, and Simon stood uneasily before the hearth. "Well, mama, what can I say? It seems scarcely sufficient to walk in after four years absence, apologise and expect to go on as before."

She looked up shrewdly at his taut features. "I wish you will not apologise at least! I was awash in a sea of remorse from your sister for weeks when *she* returned."

"How is she mama? What happened to her?" Simon asked quickly.

"You had no letter from me?"

Her son looked surprised. "Letters? No, none. Nor did I look to get any."

The Dowager sighed. "When Amelia came home I judged that a continued silence would be to no purpose and I wrote." She looked sharply at him. "You are aware, I collect, that she was never legally wed to that scoundrel?"

His lordship looked shamefaced and before he had time to find the right words, his mother spoke again.

"Lord, you are a great dunderhead!" she said, shaking her head ruefully. "But I suspected that might be the way of it. Well, to her lasting credit, Amelia stood by the wastrel. I wanted a search made for her in the beginning, but Branthorpe said no, she would soon be home again. But she wasn't. Now she doesn't speak of Morley much; indeed, I have tried to encourage her to forget the past as much as possible. Her ill-usage stemmed from the conditions she was compelled to share with him more than any actual maltreatment at his hands. He had been turned off by his family—for his constant gambling debts. Fittingly enough he died for a wager; £300 for drinking three gills of spirit and a £100 for every one consumed over that."

"Good God, the gibbet is too good for whatever bedlamite proposed that!" ejaculated his lordship, horrified.

"Well, whoever it was, the wager was taken, and a pint drunk before Mr. Morley passed into a coma. He died only hours later. Amelia knew nothing of it at her lodgings until a Bow Street Runner brought the news to her." The Dowager paused, and smiled rather sadly. "The Runner, bless him, was a fatherly soul and prevailed upon her to return home."

Simon still looked anxious. "And she really is unscathed by all this?"

His mother nodded. "She has shown a quite remarkable resilience," she said, not answering his question directly. "I am persuaded that your presence will improve her spirits more than anything. She has felt a great guilt for what she did."

Simon, who was just settling back into the deep

cushioned sofa, looked up. "But that's monstrous," he cried angrily, "and I trust you told her so."

"Oh, I did, never fear! The blame rested squarely on your shoulders, but let us leave the matter now," the Dowager commanded. "You can enlighten me instead about your recent conduct, which has given rise to such rumours."

His lordship lifted his dark brows. "Rumours?" he echoed, but could say no more as the door behind him was flung open, and an ireful voice rang out. "Ma'am, what is this I hear about my ramshackle brother?"

Mr. Frensham stood on the threshold in his mud-be-spattered gaiters and shooting jacket. His fowling-piece had been jettisoned, fortunately it seemed.

"John," warned the Dowager instantly, in an attempt to curb further animadversions on Simon's character.

His lordship, hitherto concealed from his brother's gaze, stood up. "And what do you hear of your ramshackle brother, John?" he asked without rancour. "But first let me say how glad I am to see you again."

John, astonished as much by Simon's faultless appearance, as by his sudden materialisation before him, pointedly ignored the hand held out to him, and stayed by the door. "You can scarcely expect me to reciprocate that sentiment," he said with an icy dignity which, in one so young, might have seemed ludicrous but for its obvious sincerity.

"John, don't be such a nodcock, I beg you," pleaded his mother.

"You must excuse me ma'am," he said, his face flushed with annoyance. "I have to go and change out of my dirt."

He stalked off and Amelia, just approaching the Blue Saloon, gave him a questioning look before she went in.

"Oh dear," she said to Simon, "he hasn't quarrelled with you already, surely?"

"Hardly," said his lordship. "I was not given the opportunity! What was it all about, mama? I collect he has taken exception to my dereliction of duty—for which I can scarcely blame him."

"It is not explained as simply as that," the Dowager replied. "He saw you in London and bore such a tale home as you never heard!"

"Oh no!" groaned her son. "Where was this?"

"Outside an hotel, I collect, with a female. I state the bare facts, you understand, without the embellishments which master John added."

His lordship's shoulder shook. "It is not to be wondered at that he should cut me!" He then explained briefly to his mother and sister what had transpired since his return to England.

As soon as he had finished, the Dowager said: "I do not scruple to tell you that there was never a moment when I doubted you Simon, although I own the evidence seemed damning when Cuffe added his contribution."

"Thank you," murmured his lordship, humbled.

"However," continued the Dowager, "as far as John is concerned I fear he has other grievances too. He is to be married, you see," she said, with an apparent *non sequitur*.

"But that's capital news," said Simon. "Who is the lady in question? Do I know her?"

Amelia answered. "No, you could not. She is the only daughter of our neighbours, the Dorvilles, who have taken over the Grange since you left. She is quite charming."

"Oh yes, that monstrosity I saw at our gates when I came in? The house, you gooscap!" elucidated Simon, seeing his sister's appalled expression.

"Oh yes," she giggled. "It is rather an eyesore isn't it?"

Simon could scarcely credit that he was actually home, and exchanging light-hearted banter with Amelia.

"If we can return to the matter in hand," said the Dowager severely. "The generous Marriage Settlement which your father intended John should have, was left all to pieces on his death, and John is feeling rather churlish about it. You will have to go into all the details with Cuffe, of course, but I am persuaded the matter could be set to rights by you now."

"Yes, I see. Small wonder the boy flew into the boughs when he saw me! Well, unless the estate has been left sadly involved, he need have no further worries on that head," his lordship declared.

"I told him it was likely you would see it thus, but I am afraid he took it badly, saying he wanted none of your charity," the Dowager explained.

"Don't fret! I fancy he will come about when he realises I am not quite the rake-hell he envisaged!" Simon said cheerfully.

NINE

THE SMALL family reunion continued in the Blue Saloon, until it was almost time to dress for dinner.

As Amelia accompanied her brother up the broad stairway, clinging to his arm as if to reassure herself he was really there at last, she told him that he was placed in his father's apartment.

"That mausoleum!" exclaimed Simon in dismay. "It surely cannot have been made ready yet?" he suggested hopefully.

"I think you will find it well enough," Amelia said, with the suspicion of a twinkle in her eye.

"I trust you may be right," her brother responded still unconvinced, when he left her at her own bed-chamber door. As he made his way through the dark-ening Long Gallery to the west wing, his footsteps echoed on the bare polished boards, a sound as nostal-gic to him as was the sight of his ancestors, as they looked down from their gilt frames.

The late Earl's vast room could scarcely be rendered snug on this December evening, but when his lordship opened the door it presented a welcoming spectacle. A fire, which seemed to be consuming a small forest, was blazing in the grate and casting a flickering glow onto the elaborate plaster ceiling, and onto the tapestries depicting bygone rustic scenes of hawking and hunting. Simon had closed the door softly behind him before he looked over to the alcove which housed the tester bed.

"Joliffe!" he cried, peering into the shadows by the bed hangings. "It is Joliffe is it not?"

"It is indeed, my lord," said that gentleman, clearing his throat nervously, "and if I may be permitted to say so, this is an occasion of great moment—"

"Spare me the speechifying, you great gudgeon, and come and shake hands! I had no notion you were still here," said his lordship, beaming at the man, ten years his senior, who had served him well throughout his Oxford days and after. Indeed Simon had often reflected that if he had consulted Joliffe before he helped Amelia elope, the ensuing events would have been very different.

Joliffe busied himself with lighting the branches of candles, and setting them about the chamber.

"I understand now," said Simon, "how this room came to be ready in time. You must have laboured like an anchor smith."

" 'Twas the Lady Amelia's idea. She said you'd be bound to be confabulating downstairs for a goodly time, and that gave us the chance to set things according to Cocker."

The Earl looked round appreciatively at his brushes and shaving tackle, his black silk knee breeches and frilled shirt, all set out as if he had been there for ever. "You have succeeded and no mistake," he informed his gratified valet. "Now, while you help me out of my boots, and into my evening dress—we still dress for dinner, I collect?—you shall tell me how it comes that you are still with us, you rogue."

"It was entirely due to the good offices of his late

lordship. I was retained to render what service I could
to himself and the Honourable John."

Offering silent thanks to his father's goodhearted-
ness, he cast a quizzical look at Joliffe as he removed a
glossy boot. "Not very taxing assignments, eh?"

"No, my lord, neither gentleman could be said to
have any Macaronic tendencies," returned Joliffe
solemnly.

"Indeed no," agreed his lordship, with a twitch of
the lips. "But I have, Joliffe?"

"That was not my intended inference, my lord, but I
must say—" protested the injured valet.

"All right, don't ride the high horse with me so
soon, I beg you. Let us agree my sartorial standards
differ a little from my worthy relations."

"Quite so, my lord. After your departure, for a brief
spell Mr. Frensham counted himself a member of the
Barouche Club gentry."

"What in thunder is that?"

"A set of feckless young gentlemen, my lord, whose
one ambition in life was to look and behave like coach-
men," explained Joliffe fastidiously.

"He grew out of it, I collect?" his lordship commented, reflecting that there were worse vices.

"Mercifully, yes, my lord," replied the valet with
some vehemence. "And then I think I can claim to
have effected a further slight improvement myself," he
continued modestly. "It dates from his betrothal—
which is not generally known yet, of course, but I'm
very relieved to see it, I can tell you," Joliffe confided,
picking up the threads of his close relationship with his
master as if he had never been away.

"Are you trying to tell me my brother has turned
into a bit of a loose fish?" asked his lordship sardonically.

"Oh no, that's pitching it a bit too strong, my lord,"

Joliffe protested, shocked. "But in the past he has shown a regrettable tendency to fix on females decidedly too long in the tooth for him. But Miss Dorville, now that's a different case altogether. A nicer young lady you'll never find. I couldn't have chosen better for him myself," he remarked, presenting the ultimate accolade.

"All's well then," said Simon, amused, "if this is his first serious attachment.

During the next half hour, Joliffe, although deploring all gossip, regaled his master with the tittle-tattle from below stairs, both past and present, and, by the time he was sent off to ascertain if Mr. Trant required his services, his lordship felt himself to be a shade firmer in the saddle.

It seemed at first that the small company for dinner was destined to be even smaller, as John did not appear until Jules' delectable fish soup *á la Rousse* was already served.

At the long table, which had great bulbous carved legs, and which would have dwarfed a room of moderate size, the Dowager and Simon were seated at each end, with Mr. Trant placed on the Dowager's right next to Amelia; and John finally took his place opposite his sister and Mr. Trant. This was Philip's first encounter with Mr. Frensham and he was interested to see how the brothers would deal together.

To Philip's dismay Mr. Frensham addressed him almost exclusively, and it quickly became plain that he was intent on ignoring his brother.

On being told that Philip had been in India nine years, John said: "So you are in way of being a nabob, are you Mr. Trant?"

"I doubt if I qualify for that title, although I think my father did—he was out there many years," Philip replied genially. "But then one always feels one should have stayed on and made one more lakh of rupees, you know!".

"And why then did you return, Mr. Trant? Not solely to nurse my son *en voyage,* I hope?" said the Dowager.

"No, the climate was the prime reason, ma'am, and it had already claimed my wife you see, some years before. Then when I saw what it was doing to your son, well—" he shrugged his shoulders. "I decided it was time *I* returned home before it was too late."

The Dowager murmured her sympathy, and Amelia turned a concerned face to him and seemed about to say something, when John cut in again.

"It's an exciting life out there, I'll wager, Sir."

Philip laughed. "Not in my experience it wasn't! A seemingly endless succession of long light days, no social life worthy of the name, and the only entertainment to be had generally was in listening to the dismal wails of the water-drawers."

"Mr. Trant was a conscientious assistant to the Commissioner with little time for excitement, as I know only too well as *his* assistant!" Simon explained.

But John continued to disregard his brother and plied Philip with endless questions about the land of the Mogul, when that gentleman, instead of expounding on the comparative merits of Arab and Irish bloodstock, would have much preferred to talk with the attractive young lady at his side. Amelia, on the other hand, was happy merely to have Simon near and content to exchange a few words with him from time to time.

When the meal had progressed to the *petites souffles au chocolat* the Dowager intervened. "John, I am persuaded that our guest has not travelled here with the sole purpose of delivering a lecture on the Orient.

Doubtless your brother will be delighted to answer your questions later," she said pointedly.

After this set-down the Honourable John did not utter for the remainder of the meal; a circumstance almost as trying as his earlier garrulity. When the cloth was removed and the ladies departed to the drawing-room, Simon decided he had no desire to preside over such an uneasy trio as this. John would have to be spoken to, but this was not the occasion. "Excuse me, gentlemen, but I must convey my thanks in person to Jules for this superb repast. Do not let my brother brow-beat you into another dissertation on India," he said lightly to Philip.

"Pray don't fret on that head! Like most people I am not averse to holding forth about my own experiences, however tedious," Philip assured them good-naturedly. "And tell your excellent chef the duck was *merveilleuse.*"

Simon, acknowledging Philip's remark and ignoring his brother's scowls, quit the dining-room. He had no qualms at leaving them together for he was sure that John was too well-bred to behave with anything but the greatest propriety towards Philip on his own, and would reserve his rancour for his brother. However, his lordship frowned when he thought of John's regrettable conduct at dinner, and determined to have matters out with him before another sun set.

With this, and a good many other problems on his mind, Simon was up betimes the following morning. By the time Amelia and Mr. Trant were breakfasting in the parlour, his lordship had already inspected the stables and the harness room. He was appalled to discover that some very fine blood and bone was suffering negligence at the hands of what had used to be a very conscientious stable staff. After rubbing his white cambric handkerchief over the flanks of the horses and finding it soiled each time, he had set the lads to work grooming every beast. He bade them pay particular attention to his own mount, Sinner. He had scarcely expected to see him still there, although was not surprised to find him sadly lacking exercise; he had been the only one able to handle this wayward gray sorrel. The depredations in the harness room he set aside for the moment, concentrating the grooms' attention on the welfare of the animals.

When he went back into the house it was just eight o'clock. He joined Amelia and Philip in the breakfast parlour and partook of some coffee; but as the pair seemed to be getting on famously without him, he repaired to the muniments room in the west wing and set to work with the steward, Featherstone, on the onerous task of disentangling his affairs.

Mr. Cuffe, whose nose had subsided now to a mere roseate glow, joined them shortly afterwards. He greeted his lordship with the utmost deference, bearing in mind the recent lamentable lapse of his clerk, but brightened when he found the Earl to have not the slightest height in his manner, and indeed seeming inclined to make light of the whole unfortunate incident.

Mr. Featherstone was delighted to see that his new young master had a business-like air that boded well for the future of Branthorpe. He said, in unusually expansive mood, to Mr. Cuffe later: "A deal more horse-sense there than in the parent—in almost all respects!" he added with a chuckle.

About eleven o'clock his lordship pushed back his chair, stretched his long legs and decided, albeit reluctantly, to leave the steward and attorney and go in search of his brother.

Amelia was just hurriedly crossing the great hall. In Branthorpe in the cold months the inhabitants had a tendency to move speedily from one room to another through the chilly vastness between.

"Have you seen John?" Simon asked her.

She turned down the corners of her pretty mouth expressively. "No, but I have a strong suspicion he is in mama's room receiving a jobation of monumental proportions," she told him softly.

"Poor John, I wanted him for well-nigh the same purpose!" laughed Simon.

"Well, you must own he has richly deserved it after his sullen display of tantrums yesterday," declared Amelia.

"Yes, but remember, Melly, he has been the Benjamin of this family for a long time now," her brother pointed out gently. "After all not every younger son has the good fortune to have *two* black sheep in the family!"

She smiled ruefully. "Perhaps not, but it seems he is very lucky even now, and has little cause to be as cross as crabs just because you have returned. He is practically betrothed to a delightful heiress, whom he declares he loves dearly—"

"But you don't believe he does, I collect," said Simon quickly, catching the slight nuance in his sister's voice.

"Well, he is rather flaunting his feelings for one truly enamoured I would have thought," she said hesitantly. "Although of course I am no expert," she added with a touch of bitterness which saddened her brother.

"Perhaps he is proud of his heiress—she does sound rather special!" commented Simon.

"Oh, I think she is," agreed Amelia readily enough. "But I expect you will meet her before the week is out. A small private dinner and rout is being given at the Grange for her coming of age."

"I shall certainly look forward to that as light relief

from my mountain of paper work. Although I warrant John would like to protect his betrothed from my depraved influence!" he declared, with a smile.

"I think mama is probably correcting some of his more lurid notions about you at this moment," she said, amused. "Look Simon, why not come riding with us? I am just going up to change and then I am taking Mr. Trant to see something of the estate."

"I'd love to, Melly, but I'm afraid you must make the best of a groom as a chaperon. John comes first this time."

As he was speaking, Amelia gave a small cry of dismay as her gold locket fell to the floor. Her brother bent to retrieve it, and before he handed it to her noticed the fine brown curl lovingly preserved in it. *Surely it could not be Frederick Morley's?* Simon was going to ask her about it but she chattered on about a faulty clasp in such an obviously embarrassed manner that, puzzled, he did not pursue the subject.

"I beg you will not keep Mr. Trant riding out in this cold too long, remember he is used to a tropical clime, not Yorkshire in the depths of winter," he adjured her.

"I promise I won't," she said. "He's a very agreeable person, is he not?"

Her brother looked pleased. "I'm glad you like him, Melly. He has been a good friend to me."

They parted and Simon repaired to the book-room, telling Stagg to send his brother in to him as soon as he emerged from the Dowager's room.

His mother's scold had evidently had a salutary effect Simon was relieved to see; and John greeted him politely, if with a certain coldness.

"There is not the smallest need to give me a wigging, sir!" John told him without delay. "It has been pointed out to me that I had the saddle on the wrong horse, and I am sorry. I trust you will accept my apologies," he added in stilted tones.

"Well of course I do, you great mutton-head," retorted his brother lightly, "and we'll have none of this sir-ring nonsense if you please. I don't recall I warranted it before I left home so I scarcely could now," he said wryly. "Come and sit down, John, we have much to discuss," he added coaxingly, still aware of some rigidity in his brother's features.

Both men were similarly attired in black riding dress and buckskin breeches, but John somehow contrived to impose the unkempt, dishevilled look, so popular with fashionable young men, upon his sombre garb. He did not take the cult so far as to include the habitual bad manners practised by those same young men, but just at this moment John felt he had been constantly provoked since his father's death. He particularly resented the false position he had been placed in by his misinterpretation of Simon's disreputable appearance in London. While this resentment seethed through him he remained standing, and was very much on his dignity.

Simon, by contrast, seemed almost relaxed leaning back in the chair, but his impeccable grooming gave him the more formal appearance. There was little outward family resemblance either, but both shared the Frensham obstinacy, mellowed in Simon's case by his experiences, but still undiminished in his young brother, as was to be made very evident in the next few minutes.

"I do not see what we can possibly have to discuss," said John sullenly.

"Well, to begin with there is your marriage—"

"Which will fare better without your interference! I am almost of age remember," flashed John.

Simon thought how fierce his brother looked with his curling military-style sidewhiskers. "Your meaning does not escape me, and I own you have no need to elope!" acknowledged his lordship mildly. "But I wish to help you in a more tangible manner."

"I want none of your charity," retorted John predictably.

"But John, it is not charity," protested Simon. "It is merely what would have fallen to you had my father not died so unexpectedly."

John was not to be appeased by that. "And why did I get such generous treatment from him?" he demanded fiercely. "It was simply to spite you; he did not want you to get anything which was not entailed to you."

"Yes, I've heard about the earlier Will he made, but that was done when he was feeling very bitter towards me. And Cuffe now assures me that, although he changed his mind recently about that, he still did intend you to have your additional income under the Marriage Settlement. It is only by a quirk of fate that he did not live to sign it. I am not proposing to make over the entire fortune to you, you know," his lordship said with a smile.

"I had not thought you were," came the testy response. "However," he continued in lofty tones, "I have no need of your franking. My future father-in-law has expressed himself satisfied with my expectations, and I would be grateful if you would do nothing to impede the immediate completion of the legalities."

Simon decided not to press matters further; John had obviously set his face against accepting anything from him. "You need have no fear on that head. Cuffe has the documents readily completed; they simply await the insertion of the new figures involved. Rest assured I shall put no obstacle in its way. I am sorry you feel like this about it, but I think I understand." He stood up. "May I wish you happy John? I believe I may have the pleasure of being introduced to your intended bride soon?"

"Oh yes," John said bleakly, "the rout."

"You are not thrown into transports by the prospect, I collect?" commented his brother.

"You haven't had the pleasure of meeting my future mother-in-law either, or you would not wonder at it," retorted John glumly.

His lordship raised his dark brows interrogatively, as he moved towards the book-room door.

"A pretentious pick-thank, that's all she is," John elaborated with such violence that Simon had to laugh. "Lord knows what airs of consequence she will give herself on Saturday; particularly if *you* put in an appearance."

"I?" echoed his astonished brother.

"Oh yes, I shall be quite cast in the shade, I assure you, if she has a genuine Earl captive in her drawing-room," John said, grim-faced at the thought.

Conscious that he had unwittingly strayed on to more dangerous ground, his lordship endeavoured to change the subject. "Well, you are not marrying *her*. What of the daughter?" he asked encouragingly, as they mounted the stairs.

"Oh, she's quite different," John told him, rather uninformatively.

"I'm relieved to hear it," murmured Simon, thinking there was an absence of rapture in his brother's voice at the mention of his beloved; but this was quickly to be rectified.

"Oh yes, she's a wonderful girl," John said with great enthusiasm, "and I love her dearly. Not exactly beautiful, I suppose. But a fine figure, as tall as I am, maybe even a bit taller," he admitted reluctantly, but with scrupulous honesty. "Rides like an angel, with a feather light hand. Can tool a phaeton and a lively pair—and handles the ribbons in prime style," he concluded with great zeal.

"Really," said Simon faintly, a picture of a huge equestrian Amazon forming irresistibly in his mind. "Under your instruction, I collect?" he asked politely, although from what he could recall of his brother's neck-or-nothing approach to the subject, considered it unlikely. He may have improved, of course, he thought charitably.

"Oh no," said John, disclaiming any such honour. "It was her capital skill on the hunting field that first attracted my attention to her."

His lordship knew not what to make of this, but reflected that at least John was conversing with him in a reasonably normal fashion. Encouraged, he said with a reminiscent smile: "Do you remember how many hours we used to spend standing on these during the holidays?" and he indicated the row of hard upright chairs lining the walls of the Long Gallery, through which they were now passing. "Solemnly practising our whip handling!"

"That's a shabby trick! You are playing on my sentiments, now," John retorted, reverting to his cold manner instantly.

"Oh, do forgive me," his lordship said gravely, but as he left John and went to his own bedchamber, he reflected that the interview had proceeded a great deal better than he had dared hope. He would broach the matter of income with John sometime in the future, when his resentment had cooled.

TEN

Mrs. Dorville was having a most gratifying week composed of frenzied bustling about and sanguine expectation; not since she had bowed to her spouse's regrettable desire to retire from Town into his native Yorkshire had she so enjoyed herself. At last she would have the opportunity to demonstrate to her neighbours her true consequence in the community; a fact she felt had hitherto not been grasped by them. When Mr. Dorville had first put forth the argument that his daughter was as likely to make an excellent catch on the matrimonial market in the fastness of the northern countryside as in the mêlée of the London season, his wife had disagreed violently. However, his preference for being a big fish in a small pool was generally beginning to be looked upon with more favour by Mrs. Dorville. Her husband, as a merchant, had always put the acquisition of money before title, and she had hoped her daughter would redress the balance by acquiring one; true, John was only an Honourable and she still regretted his reduced circumstances, but she was more than compensated by her growing association with Branthorpe Park.

When the chef rode over from the Park on Saturday morning, and Ann was unfortunately in York with her father, Mrs. Dorville felt she had managed the difficult occasion rather skilfully. However, this was due in fact to Jules's volatile temperament being quite overborne by the combined effect of Mrs. Dorville's insensitive approach to the religion of cooking, and her very alien modern kitchen. As that awesome English lady enumerated briskly on her fingers: "turbot, eels, dorics, saddle of mutton, sirloin of beef, fowl, tongue and ham," he bore this barbaric cornucopia with equanimity, thinking of the delicious sauces and embellishments he could prepare for each; but his spirit was quite broken when she added her preference that these dishes should be accompanied by boiled potatoes and other nourishing roots, the whole enlivened with pickles.

He had returned, seething with rebellion to Branthorpe Park, only to discover that his original employer was coming home suddenly. Jules seized on this event at first as an excuse for refusing the outside work, and decided to enlist my lord's support in the matter. However, when his temper had cooled, he quickly realised that the Earl would be too pre-occupied with his own problems to be concerned over such a trivial matter, and he stoically resigned himself to doing his best in decidedly adverse circumstances. He was helped in this resolve by a very satisfactory idea for a small revenge on Mrs. Dorville, as he gloomily contemplated her suggested menu.

Mr. Dorville was not much in evidence during the week preceding the celebration; he kept to his study, and whenever Ann went to him she found he was engrossed in figure work and papers. She thought he looked worried.

"Papa, are you quite certain about the arrangements with Mr. Frensham?" she asked him on one occasion.

"Mm?" he said, looking up at her over his glasses.

"The Marriage Settlement. You really are satisfied with it now?" Ann reiterated.

"Well of course I am, kitten," he assured her heartily. As always, she tried not to wince at this endearment which, like so many parental notions, was woefully unsuitable; whatever her faults, she could not be called kittenish. "You seemed to be rather preoccupied with your accounts, that's all," she told him.

He gave a theatrical wink. "I think you will find I will be less preoccupied with them next week—at least until the provision bills start to come in for the festal board of course!" he said with a chuckle.

His daughter was relieved to hear that he was simply keeping out of harm's—or more accurately her mother's—way, until the preparations for the weekend function were over, because Ann herself was feeling happy now at the way everything was going. The fact that she was less than a sennight from being in command of her fortune contributed surprisingly little to her contentment. Her needs were few, and although she was realistic enough to see that John would be in control of her funds in a matter of months, she considered they would be more than adequate to support their life in Lincolnshire. That her husband would spend a sizeable sum on the maintenance of his stables was to be expected, and she preferred he should do that rather than fritter it away on the gambling tables of Watier's or the Dandy Club. It was true that for a brief time after John's sudden declaration of love, she had doubted his motives but, thinking about it, she decided that it had been the obvious moment for him to select as it was the first time he had seen her since the marriage was definitely settled.

Now she was looking forward to running an establishment of her own, for an idle life, such as she enjoyed at the Grange, was not really to her taste. It could scarcely be described as idle on the eve of her birthday, however. Her mother had left in the carriage that morning for York, taking their maid with her to carry the innumerable items of food, and such things as surplus bunches of playing cards, which she was convinced they lacked even after a week of laying in stocks. Her other missions included a check on the arrangements, already quite adequately made by Mr. Dorville on his visit to York, for the engagement of a musical trio, and a visit to her coiffeuse. Ann did not look to see her back until late afternoon, and could not suppress a sigh of relief at her departure. With the help of the harassed, but equally relieved remaining staff and Jules, who was due to come down from Branthorpe again that afternoon, Ann hoped to put the final touches to the preparations in peace.

In the lesser half of the drawing-room, which was to be used initially for dining tomorrow night, Ann was going over yet again the placing of the twelve diners, when she heard horse's hooves in the drive and assumed it was the chef arriving. She was surprised, therefore, when the manservant came in and announced that Mr. Frensham had called.

"Show him in here, please Prickett," Ann requested, hoping that the evident chaos she was in would deter a lengthy visit. It was a sennight since her ride with John and his sister, and subsequently she had heard nothing from the Park; nor had she expected to, as she had not fixed to ride with Amelia this week, and she hazarded that John would wish to avoid being involved in the pre-ball arrangements.

"It's very nice to see you, John," she said with a slight feeling of shyness as she recalled their last meeting. "Although I own I thought you were Jules!" she added lightly.

John cast a wild look about the festive drawing-room. "Oh Lord, it's not today is it?" he asked fearfully.

"Good heavens no!" she laughed. "Things will scarcely be ready by tomorrow." Ann thought he looked a bit uneasy, so she stopped hovering by the table and went to sit by the fire. "Is all well at Branthorpe?" she asked, as he paced aimlessly towards the window.

"Oh yes, that is—well, that's what I came to see you about in part. I should have come earlier, I suppose. You haven't heard anything then?" he said incoherently, and turned towards her suddenly.

"Heard what?" Ann repeated, puzzled. Surely there could be no change in their betrothal plans again or her father would have been informed?

"It's my brother, he's come home without warning—like a thief in the night," he informed her in grumpy tones.

"Your brother," Ann said blankly, but conscious she was parroting everything he said in a stupid manner. "From India you mean?" He nodded, and she started to say: "That's wonderful news, isn't it?" but finished in failing accents remembering her guilty eavesdropping on John's arrival at Branthorpe from London, and his vituperations on his brother. So he had been right, he *had* seen his brother. She felt hot and uncomfortable.

"Well, I think it was shabby of him not to have given us more warning. It has thrown everything into such a tumult," John complained crossly.

Ann endeavoured to disregard this remark and her own confusion concerning this event, and offered, as warmly as possible, an invitation to the brother to attend the dinner. Only that morning an extra female had been added to one guest's party but that was for the dance afterwards, and not the dinner, so it would not help her seating arrangements, she reflected rapidly.

"Thank you," said John, evidently relieved that he had not had to petition on his brother's behalf. "He would like that, oh—and there's a friend with him, too, I'm afraid, a Mr. Trant," he added, in a voice suggesting this was yet another reprehensible act of his brother.

"Well then, he must come too," Ann offered politely, thinking that at least it would spare them sitting down thirteen to dinner.

A little belatedly, remorse seemed to overtake Mr. Frensham. "I do apologise for not telling you all this before, Ann. He's been home almost a week now, but things have been going a-pace with the Settlement and I wanted to be able to tell you everything was definitely completed."

"And is it?"

"Yes, Cuffe told me last night and he left to return to London today. Now isn't that capital news?" he asked her excitedly. "We can make our final plans for the wedding. I thought about the end of February. The first three months of mourning will be over by then, and in the meantime I can go down to Wragston and set things in order there—" He paused for breath at that point, and came towards her.

"John, I beg you!" Ann pleaded, laughing and holding up her hand in protest. "Is there need for such haste? It is going to be very bleak for the wedding tour in February is it not?" she asked, snatching at the first objection which occurred to her.

"Wedding tour?" he echoed, with a vacant look. "Oh yes, don't fret, we'll soon fix something," he went on hastily. "There's no end of relations who'd be delighted to provide a house, I shouldn't wonder," he told her blithely.

"Yes, but supposing the roads are impassable, and they often are in February, you know. Why we may not be able to get to Wragston even," she protested, unwilling to be hustled into a hasty marriage.

John acknowledged that she had a point there, but refused to be deterred. "No need to look on the black side, eh?" he responded bracingly.

With her mind quite dazed with last minute problems for her birthday celebrations, Ann did not feel equal to the task of planning her wedding at the same time. "Let's leave it for the moment, John, please," she said, looking pleadingly at him from under her long dark lashes. "There is no call for any *Gazette* announcement because of the mourning, so nothing final need be fixed on," she entreated him.

John looked down at his betrothed in some alarm. "I say, you're not crying off, are you? I couldn't bear that."

He said this so earnestly that Ann felt quite touched. "No, I promise I shan't do that," she told him unequivocally.

With an impetuous movement he took her hand. "Thank you, I shall keep you to that," he said softly.

Prickett seemed to appear almost instantly. Ann removed her hand slowly from John's grip.

"The cook's 'ere, miss," Prickett proclaimed, in what were probably meant to be impartial tones, but which sounded full of reproof to Ann's ears. She felt a certain sympathy for the servant as he did not know of her betrothal, and her behaviour in entertaining John alone did, no doubt, seem quite improper to him.

"Will you excuse me now?" she asked, rising. "There really is a host of things I must do."

"Surely. Well, till tomorrow then," he said, making his way towards the disapproving Prickett.

"Yes, and I look forward to meeting your brother," Ann replied with more courtesy than truth.

She wished it had been possible to ask John more about his brother, but she suspected he disapproved of him so much that she would not be given an unbiased picture. The only word of his earlier description of him which sprang to her mind was "dissipated", which reassured her not at all; she could not help wondering if her party was doomed to disaster. With sinking spirits, she reflected that it was very unfortunate that the Earl of Branthorpe should have chosen her birthday of all days on which to make his spectacular debut in the neighbourhood. To add to her despondency she noticed a few very fine snowflakes drifting down outside the window.

ELEVEN

FAR FROM throwing everything in to a tumult at Branthorpe, as his brother had claimed, Simon had spent a gruelling week endeavouring to set to rights Branthorpe affairs. That they had been neglected was only too clear; but the Earl did not lay the blame at John's door; it was, after all, only a month since his father's death and the decline was of longer duration than that. His mother, though, had given Simon to understand that John, whilst enjoying the status of an elder son in recent years, had shown no inclination to fulfil the duties of one; again Simon could not find it in him to blame John.

What he did regard as reprehensible was the state of affairs in the stables and coach house, for he had imagined that at least John would take an interest in those. He had discovered the travelling coach—soon to be paid for at last, he reflected—in a direful state; the leather straps upon which the whole weight of the body rested were in a perilous way. His lordship caused it to be sent to nearby Pocklington, where the wheelwright and saddlesmith found themselves suddenly with a vast amount of work to be done for Branthorpe Park.

Simon refrained from taking his brother to task over these matters as he had no wish to aggravate John's bad feelings towards him. He would be married soon, and was obviously intent on removing himself to Wragston at the first opportunity. His lordship had resolved to present two of the best hunters in the stables to John and his bride as wedding gifts; the rest of the blood cattle he meant to sell before he set about establishing his own more modest stables.

When Mr. Cuffe had to be conveyed to York on the Friday morning to catch the Mail for London, Simon found an antiquated landaulet, belonging to his mother, to be the only roadworthy vehicle. After a week of being cooped up in the house, he decided, in spite of the frosty weather, to drive Cuffe himself. He had used to be a fine whip and longed to get his hand in again. Philip elected at the last moment to accompany them; he needed to purchase some dancing shoes for the following evening. Simon warned him that, even with the hood up, the demi-landau would not be very snug, but well wrapped around with rugs he and Mr. Cuffe contrived to keep warm. His lordship, seated on the box in front, enjoyed himself so much tooling along the familiar road that he scarcely noticed the icy temperature.

When the attorney and his portmanteau had been deposited at the Mail offices to await the coach—a parting on both sides of mutual relief that their respective work was completed satisfactorily—Simon directed the bays towards the Swan. Recognition was instantaneous when the ostler came forward, and Simon saw he need have no qualms for his horses' welfare. He and Philip went into the coffee-room to restore their circulation while the horses were baited.

It was not market day, and they secured fire-side seats in the deserted parlour. Simon called "house" after removing his thick caped driving coat and depositing his gloves on the seat. When the landlord had put two brandies before them, his lordship was the first to speak.

"I'm very pleased you have decided to stay on, Philip," he told his friend. "Your mother really does not mind?"

Philip chuckled. "In her letter she sounded so awe-struck to hear of your sudden elevation to the peerage that I think she would be prepared to spare me indefinitely. However, I do intend to return to Lyme by Christmas, and shall be fixed in London again in January."

"I fear you may have found it rather tedious at Branthorpe. I have been a somewhat neglectful host," Simon said apologetically.

"Oh, indeed I have not," Philip declared with fervour. "Lady Amelia has shown me the utmost complacence. She is a delightful creature."

Simon could not fail to notice the rapt expression on

his friend's countenance as he said this. It confirmed what he had half-suspected from that first dinner at Branthorpe; Philip had fallen in love with Amelia. Nothing would have pleased Simon more than to be able to welcome him into the family, but he was uneasy about Amelia. He could not quite define why he should be so, but she seemed—well—distracted, he supposed. And there was the locket; that was a bit of a mystery, too. He had almost taxed his mother on the subject, for she surely must know what it signified, but he was not extremely cautious about seeming to pry into his sister's secrets. He would have to wait until they saw fit to tell him. However because of this doubt, he felt unable to encourage Philip as he would have liked.

His lordship merely replied: "Yes, she is. And speaking of delightful creatures, I see none here today upon which to feast our eyes."

"No, but I did wonder if it were a coincidence when you chose to come here again," responded Philip slyly.

Simon admitted nothing on this score, as he was confident that if the Vision lived hereabouts he would surely have little difficulty in discovering her name, and the following day would provide him with the opportunity.

"I own I am looking forward to meeting my neighbours and future in-laws tomorrow, although they sound a formidable tribe! A toadying dragon of a mama with a hardriding daughter of mammoth proportions, I collect," his lordship explained with some relish. "That is if my brother is to be believed."

Philip's dark eyes kindled appreciatively. "Is that how he describes his future bride? Well, there is no romantical blindness there it seems."

"No, he cherishes no illusions evidently, and yet vows quite passionately he loves her," declared the

Earl. "I shall do all I can to encourage the match I assure you! Even Branthorpe is scarcely spacious enough to contain us both indefinitely, and I cannot see him residing at Wragston on his own, and industriously managing the estate."

"Is Lady Branthorpe one of the party tomorrow?" Philip asked presently.

"No, it seems she gladly took the excuse of my father's recent death to decline the dragon's invitation. I am charged with the role of chaperon to Amelia—a confidence that I hope this time is not misplaced. However, I am happy to attend the assembly simply as an observer, and shall not be sorry to forego the dancing after my fatiguing week. And I fancy it will be a rewarding gathering," he added optimistically.

A look of disappointment crossed Philip's face. "No, of course, none of you may dance because of the mourning. I had quite forgotten."

"Don't despair," recommended Simon, on seeing his doleful countenance. "I am told that Amelia and John are to be permitted one or two dances. After all, I suspect my father would have been the last person to set store by any such niceties."

Simon had one or two commissions to carry out for his mother in the town, so the two friends soon had to quit the warmth of the inn. The Earl's acquaintance had been legion in the area, and it seemed they were destined to meet a multitude of them that morning. It was in Micklegate that Simon recognised the familiar features of the squire, whose land marched with his; the two old friends checked suddenly, momentarily blocking the flagway. Philip walked on, taking the opportunity to look in a print shop window.

Almost at once a young girl of short stature carrying a veritable mountain of parcels cannoned into Simon's back.

"Maria! Do you look where you are going, you clumsy dolt of a girl!" bellowed a powerful female voice in his lordship's ear. He turned round, apologised to the maidservant—for such she obviously was—who had collided with him, and started to pick up the parcels for her. The girl was by this time scarlet with confusion and misery, but her mistress continued to mingle obsequious regrets to Simon with violent animadversions on her servant's character.

His lordship cut across this tasteless rhetoric. "Madam, I beg you, do not put yourself about!" he rapped out. "The fault was entirely mine and I offer you my sincere regrets." He then turned to the maid and said kindly: "I hope you sustained no hurt from your stumble."

She shook her head silently, speech seemingly beyond her powers for the moment.

"Good day to you both then," said his lordship, raising his hat and, inclining his bow a little more towards the maid than her mistress, turned his attention back to the squire, who had done no more in the episode than retrieve a particularly adventurous package.

"Odious woman," said Simon who, still annoyed by the incident, made no effort to moderate his resonant voice.

The squire looked at him curiously. "You don't know her yet, then?"

"No, should I?" asked his lordship.

"Well, she is your neighbour—Mrs. Dorville, you know."

"By Jupiter, really?" roared Simon, and laughed so heartily that Philip looked round from his study of the prints. "Well squire, that should make for fine sport at her daughter's ball tomorrow night! No doubt I shall see you there?"

The squire, who had quietly enjoyed the encounter,

said he would certainly be there with his good lady and their two younkers.

His lordship enquired politely of the squire's wife and the boys, and explained simply that he had returned home from India due to ill-health, he then rejoined Philip who was anxious to know what all the fuss was about. Their progress through the town continued to be impeded by a series of astonished old friends, and Simon became quite weary of repeating the brief explanation of his sudden return. At last they gained the premises of his lordship's cordwainer, and Philip had the good fortune to be supplied with a splendid pair of old-fashioned silver buckled shoes of perfect fit.

The remainder of the visit was uneventful, and by two o'clock they were in the sturdy but ancient landaulet again, rattling along the dry frozen road to Branthorpe. A few sparse flakes of snow started to fall as they approached the hamlet, but not enough to impair Simon's vision. About a quarter of a mile ahead there were two galloping riders; they gradually disappeared into the distance, and his Lordship was unable to distinguish their identity. But he hoped at least they would look to their horses' welfare when they arrived at their destination, or their mounts would doubtless take a chill.

When he drove into the Branthorpe stable yard, having dropped a shivering Philip at the front porch, he found the two horses to be his own responsibility.

Matthew, the elderly groom, could be seen through the open stable doors, still unsaddling the second horse in his slow, deliberate fashion.

"Come Matt," enjoining his lordship briskly, jumping down from the driving box, "there'll be plenty of rugs needed. Where are they?"

"Aye, now let's think," said the groom, and stopped work altogether to scratch his head.

"Oh, no matter," said Simon impatiently. "What's happened to the stable lads?"

"I bet owt y'like they be int' tack room," cackled the room in a confidential manner. "Ay, and now I think on, that's weer t'blankets be an'all."

Acting swiftly on his hard won information, Simon burst into the saddle room and put four lads, enjoying an uproarious game of cards, to instant flight.

"Stir your stumps, you sluggards! Didn't you hear the carriage! Fetch rugs to the stables this minute!"

When all four horses were blanketed, he asked Matthew about the two saddle horses.

"Ay, m'lord," the groom responded, showing a somewhat belated respect, " 'twere m'lady Amelia and Miss Betsy—just back afore you they wus."

"I see. Thank you, Matt. And don't forget that the carriage has to be fetched from Pocklington in the morning. We shall need it later."

"Oh no, m'lord," said Matt, offended. "I'd not forget owt like that, now woulda?"

Simon smiled to himself and went into the house.

* * *

At dinner that night John mentioned his visit to Shipton Grange and confirmed that his brother and Mr. Trant would be very welcome there the following evening.

"And a merry meeting it is like to be," said Simon grinning. "I had what could only be termed an unfortunate encounter with the redoubtable Mrs. Dorville today, and I'm not at all sure *I* shall be particularly welcome."

John glared at him. "Now what have you done?" he

demanded crossly, as one who suffered infinite wrong
at the hands of his brother.

Simon explained.

"I might have known you'd do something mutton-
headed like that!" John snapped. "If you queer my
pitch there, you'll answer for it."

"Oh really, that's doing it a brown, isn't it?" chided
his brother mildly. "You said yourself what a ter-
magant the woman is."

"Maybe," John conceded grudgingly, "but there's no
call to heap abuse on her head the minute you set eyes
on her—in front of the squire, too," he added, as if
that were the last straw.

"He enjoyed it enormously, I fancy," Simon assured
him blithely.

"Oh, I don't doubt it, but it is not to be supposed
that Mrs. Dorville did," John retorted.

The Dowager, although not unamused by this tale,
decided to turn the subject and enquired of the squire's
health from Simon.

Amelia had been talking with Mr. Trant about
York, but when the opportunity arose Simon spoke to
her.

"What was the great hurry this afternoon, Melly?"

She looked at him wide-eyed. "Hurry? Where?"

"Well, you and Betsy were galloping in front of me
when I came home as if there was a devil at your
heels," Simon said.

Amelia gave an odd little smile, and it seemed to Simon that, in the light of the candelabra before her, her
face was a little pinker than before. "Oh well, it was
beginning to snow and I wanted to get home as quickly
as possible."

Simon's question had been posed quite casually, but
he noticed the guarded look on Amelia's face and he
was surprised when his mother intervened at this point.

"Amelia was carrying out a small commission for me, Simon. Sir William Lambert is a martyr to the gout, you know," said the Dowager in sympathetic tones, which surprised her son again, as he had not thought there to be any particular bond of amity between the Frenshams and the Lamberts. "Only the other day," his mother continued, "I discovered a bottle of the excellent nostrum prescribed for your father in Town by Dr. Baillie. I thought it would be a kindness to send it over to Kerswell for Sir William."

"Indeed yes," murmured a bemused Simon, although this was the first he had heard of his father's gout; perhaps he had suffered a decline in his later years? There was so much still he did not know, he reflected, and this was hardly the occasion to pursue the matter. "I'm sorry you had to ride out in such weather, Melly, but I suppose that was my fault for taking the only roadworthy carriage," he said, and thought it odd in his mother not to have sent the remedy by a footman with an explanatory note.

The ladies withdrew, presently, and left the three gentlemen to their port. John, although still willing to find fault with his brother whenever he had the opportunity, was prepared to converse with him now, albeit rather coolly; he had wearied of discussing India with Mr. Trant some days ago.

The conversation was still somewhat desultory and soon Simon bade the footman hand him a package from the side table. His lordship unwrapped a small framed print.

"I purchased this in York today, John. I was uncertain of what kind of gift to present to Miss Dorville tomorrow as I have not yet met her, but will this serve, do you suppose?" He propped the picture up for his brother's inspection against the huge silver epergne.

John scarcely glanced at the colourful scene of a

hunt and hounds in full cry. "How should I know? I should not have thought it necessary to give her anything," he said in an off-hand manner.

"But dash it, John, she is my future sister-in-law!" protested his lordship.

"Let us hope so," retorted his brother in accusatory tones. "But I tell you frankly, I wish you were not coming with us tomorrow."

"Oh, but I wouldn't miss it for the world!" Simon assured him mischievously.

"How are we to get there, since you have seen fit to disperse all the carriages?" demanded John.

"Don't fret on that head! Everything is taken care of," said his lordship with maddening calm.

"Well, don't look to me for any assistance in retrieving them. I shall be going into York at first light in the morning." After delivering this shot he drained his glass and departed.

Philip, who was getting accustomed to these fraternal brangles, said casually: "One would almost think he was jealous of you, although I fail to see how he should be as you haven't met the lady in question."

"No," said Simon, with an amused gleam in his eye. "I think in this instance, the explanation is more straightforward than that! I'll wager he has forgotten to buy the damsel a present himself. Hence the sudden trip to York!"

Philip smiled. "I believe you may be right. He looked quite furious when you mentioned the matter of a gift."

"My little brother, I suspect, is quite capable of looking furious whenever I mention any subject at the moment!" said his lordship sardonically, as he returned the offending print to its wrappings. "I could wish his was a forgiving disposition like Melly's."

"Oh yes, Lady Amelia," said Philip, with his usual

ingenuous enthusiasm whenever her name arose, which Simon found quite breathtaking in his customarily stolid friend. "She has such an open temper. It is not to be supposed that she will remain unattached for long," he said lightly, but he had a white-knuckled grip on his glass's stem on the table before him. "And I see she wears a locket constantly—or is that her late husband's?"

Judging by the sudden tenseness of Philip's plump features, Simon could hazard how much it had cost him to ask such a question, and he was a little dismayed by it. "If I knew the answer, my dear Philip, I should tell you gladly. I own to a certain amount of speculation about that locket myself."

"I should not have mentioned it, forgive me. It is no concern of mine," said Philip hastily.

From the head of the table, Simon regarded his friend steadily over interlaced fingers. "Is the locket the sum of your misdoubts?"

"I'm not sure I should say more if she had not confided in you," murmured Philip, meeting Simon's gaze at last, but with troubled brown eyes.

"Well, I shan't press you, of course, but I do feel some uneasiness about her myself," Simon confessed. "I had thought it to be imagination for she has not a secretive nature, but I hazard that my mother has instructed that I shall not be told of this attachment until all is settled. Their caution is understandable I suppose, but rather foolish. My reputation as a meddler is not going to be easily scotched, I fear," said his lordship in rueful accents. "Why my brother is obviously in daily expectation of my putting a period to his betrothal by my ineptitude!"

Philip, by this time, was too uncomfortably aware of his own ineptitude in having unguardedly laid bare his feelings to take heed of what his friend was saying.

"Before we leave the subject," he said quickly, in an attempt to retrieve the situation, "you understand that I mooted this question simply out of concern for your sister's happiness."

Simon, who perceived his friend to be floundering deeper and deeper into confusion, endeavoured to alleviate his misgivings by saying in prosaic tones: "Of course! And I am indebted to you for making known your suspicions—they reinforce my own and I am resolved to place them before my mother at the first opportunity."

That opportunity arose the same evening, when the rest of the company had retired early to recruit their energies for the festivities the following day, and Simon and the Dowager were left sitting over the dying embers of the fire in the drawing-room; but he did not have to raise the subject, the Dowager did so first.

"You must allow me to know best where Amelia is concerned you know," she said, fixing shrewd eyes on her son.

Simon remained silent, only raising his dark brows in enquiry.

"She is not skilled at deception, as I am persuaded you observed at dinner tonight. My tale did not hoax you either, I fancy, but I did not wish you to question Amelia further."

"But consider, ma'am," urged Simon, "this mystery, whatever it may be, cannot be concealed for ever. In fact it must be known to others already. What about John for instance? And the maid Betsy?" he demanded, his long jawline set stubbornly.

The Dowager nodded, apparently unmoved by this logic. "Yes, but they are the only ones. Your father knew, of course," she told him calmly. "John is too absorbed with his own problems to interfere although I knew he does not approve of the situation, and Betsy is sworn to secrecy."

Simon reflected that both courses of information were effectively closed to him; John would certainly not tell him anything at the moment, and he could scarcely approach a servant on the matter. Which left only his mother, so he resumed his attack.

"If my father knew of this—affair, liaison or whatever—it must be of several months standing," Simon argued impatiently, and hurled a log into the grate, causing a cloud of grey ash to fly up the chimney.

"It is as you say, a long-standing dilemma," his mother agreed carefully. "I own I have been weak because of your father's death intervening, else the matter would have been terminated some weeks ago. It will undoubtedly cause your sister some distress, but I am persuaded she is stout enough to face it now."

Simon listened grim-faced and with increasing misgiving to this unhelpful speech, which seemed to indicate that his mother considered Amelia's choice of partner unacceptable. "This is monstrous ma'am! I am entitled to know what is going on under my own roof!" he declared in wrathful accents.

The Dowager looked at her son sympathetically. "I'm sorry Simon. I am fully aware that you would not wish your sister to suffer unnecessarily, and that is why I do not want you influencing her at the moment. It is better she should grieve a little now than ruin the whole of the rest of her life."

"I thought I had already helped her to do that once," retorted Simon with some bitterness. "Is she now to have no say in her own affairs? She is of age, remember. How can you be so sure you are right this time?" For a brief moment he thought the shaft had struck home; a look of uncertainty and sadness passed over his mother's face.

When she spoke though, he voice was firm. "You *must* believe I am right Simon. I shall act upon my decision once the Dorville ball is over, and then you shall be told."

An unwelcome thought struck Simon. "But Amelia is in my care tomorrow night. Am I not to know at least who is involved?"

"Oh you need suffer no qualms on that head," his mother asserted placidly. "It is not to be supposed that Amelia would give you the smallest grounds for anxiety on such an occasion."

The Dowager then stood up slowly, with much rustling of black silk, and bade her perturbed son goodnight.

When she had gone Simon sank back into his chair; his chin bent as low as the stiff points of his collar would permit, and stared abstractedly at the yellow flames now curling round the solitary log.

The groom of the chambers coming in later to dowse the lights and make safe the fire thought him asleep; but when his lordship turned a blank gaze upon him, the groom said impudently—for he had been in m'lord's service since that young gentleman wore skirts—"Had it been a bear it would have bitten you, m'lord!"

"Ay," acknowledged Simon with a sardonic smile, and getting stiffly to his feet and stretching, "and it may yet, Nokes, it may yet!"

TWELVE

THE SNOW of the previous day had disappeared by the morning of Ann's birthday and, with that worry removed, she was apprehensive only of the effect that John's brother and his friend might have on the gathering that evening. Ann hoped John would not quarrel with his brother, and that the unknown friend would not—like his lordship—be "dissipated." Perhaps they would both get foxed on her father's generous cellar? Another minor problem had exercised her ingenunity for, try as she may, it had seemed unavoidable that Lady Amelia and Ralph Lambert should be placed side by side at dinner. Since observing her friend that day when Amelia had rejoined John and herself after visiting Kerswell, Ann had become quite convinced that the explanation must lie in some attachment between Amelie and Ralph. However, as this was obviously clandestine she wished she might avoid throwing them upon each other's company in public.

But all speculation upon the forthcoming celebration was quelled for a time when Ann received an exceptionally magnificent gift from her father—a parure of necklace, ear-bobs and a bracelet made up of diamonds of a size to make her doubt that they were real. Her father left her in no uncertainty on this point though, and added: "They're in the way of an investment you might say, kitten. For you, just in case." Ann was a little puzzled by the remark, bearing in mind that she took command of a fortune that very day. Perhaps this purchase was what her father had been brooding over during the past week?

By seven-fifteen that evening Ann was already dressed with the help of the nimble-fingered Maria and she went to her mother's boudoir. On seeing her daughter through the dressing-table mirror, Mrs. Dorville leapt to her feet scattering scent bottles and sundry jars in all directions. "My love, you look positively ravishing!" she cried ecstatically, throwing out her arms in a Siddons-like gesture. "But the ear-rings—and the bracelet, where are they?" she demanded, her critical faculties returning somewhat abruptly.

Ann had spent most of the day in conflict with her mother over wearing the diamonds, and also over the unfashionable dressing of her hair; the latter was a longstanding wrangle. She had compromised by wearing the necklace only, but had positively refused, as always, to relinquish her smooth hair style for any striving after face-framing curls à la Titus so beloved by her parent and the fashion magazines. Now, in a rich blue silk, low-cut dress with tiny puff sleeves and a single deep flounce about the hem, with no head dress save a fillet of silver thread keeping her hair in place, Ann felt that the necklace was shown to best advantage. The only concession to mourning for the late Earl, by both Dorville ladies on this occasion, was confined to the wearing of black gloves.

"I don't deny you look quite exquisite," continued Mrs. Dorville, "but think what a foil that black is for the bracelet!"

"Oh, very well, mama," conceded Ann, reluctant but anxious to keep the peace. "But I will not countenance ear-rings!"

Before going to put on the bracelet she helped her mother secure the elaborate turban of emerald velvet and matching curled feathers which complemented her velvet gown of the same arresting shade.

Ann hoped that her sycophantic mama, who had been delighted the the previous evening when she returned from York to hear that Lord Branthorpe was returned and would be present at their rout, would not behave too outrageously towards him.

"My love," said Mrs. Dorville slowly, surveying her own reflection with evident satisfaction. "A simply famous notion came to me as I lay sleepless last night," she went on with enthusiasm, then peered less complacently into the mirror. "I really can't think why I haven't got the most dreadful circles beneath my eyes today," she added.

Her mother often declared herself a martyr to wakeful nights, although any such affliction was denied by her spouse who merely complained ungallantly of her tendency to snore. So Ann was not perturbed by this confession, but the arch tone of voice did worry her in no small measure.

"And what would that be mama?" she asked, casting an anxious eye to her mother's watch on the dressing-table. *Past seven-thirty, the first dinner guests may arrive at any moment.*

Mrs. Dorville swung round on the stool to face her daughter. "Well, as you know," she began in confidential tones, "John is a good enough boy in his way but it would be splendid, would it not, if you were to fix the Earl's attentions?"

Ann, who was not easily discomposed by her mama, stared down at her round-eyed and speechless.

"It is not to be supposed it could be accomplished swiftly, of course," she went on thoughtfully. "But first you could cry-off from your present betrothal. After all there is no denying that John's expectations have sunk lamentably of late—and then in a few—"

"Mama!" cried Ann, recovering her powers of speech at last. "I beg you will not put forward such improper proposals—even in jest."

Mrs. Dorville looked hurt. "I vow I was never more serious, my love."

"Pray consider, mama, how am I to receive my guests with even tolerable composure when you make outrageous suggestions like this? Why, they are virtually at the door!" Ann protested in anguished tones.

"But I merely wanted to ensure that you treat the Earl with the utmost complaisance, and do nothing which might frustrate the success of any further scheme. I know you have taken it unaccountably into your head that his lordship is not quite the thing," declared Mrs. Dorville peevishly.

"I think it is time we went down, mama," Ann said severely, not trusting herself to further discussion on the matter.

"My goodness, so it is," her mother acknowledged, picking up the watch and pinning it to her much-ornamented bosom. "But do you remember that bracelet, my love," she called imperturbably to Ann's rigid departing back.

*   *   *

It was almost ten o'clock before Ann had a quiet moment to herself. She stood for a time in the card room behind her mother's chair, ostensibly watching the play, but in fact she was trying to assess how the evening was progressing. Undoubtedly from the guests' point of view the party seemed a success. In spite of bitter cold weather everyone had arrived except for the Winthorpes—a family with a universal passion for horses, whom she thought John would appreciate. From her own viewpoint, though, the evening had not been entirely enjoyable. The discovery that Lord Branthorpe was the gentleman she had already encountered in the Swan had done nothing to help her treat him with the coolness she had intended after her mother's alarming statements immediately before the guests' arrival. Indeed, over dinner, although her mother had predictably occupied most of Lord Branthorpe's attention, Ann had found it impossible to resist his charm.

Then, recalling her subsequent foolishness, she felt hot and uncomfortable, although the card room was cool compared with the ballroom she had just quitted. Her intention at dinner had been merely to relieve Lord Branthorpe of the necessity of answering her mother's increasingly importuning questions with a request to pass a dish of innocuous-looking pâté. On the recommendation of the Earl, Mrs. Dorville had helped herself to a substantial portion, and when mother and daughter were sampling this *specialité* of Jules, Lord Branthorpe informed them, not without a certain relish it seemed to Ann, that snails had always been a favourite of his and he was pleased they shared his taste. Even as she remembered the incident, a feeling of queasiness assailed Ann, but at the time her mother's obvious anguish had caused his lordship's quizzical gaze to meet her own and she had at once been transported back to that first exchange of amused looks at the posting-house. Cross with herself for not being more distant with his lordship, she had turned her attention to John, who had behaved in the most charming manner imaginable all evening. Thenceforth, the conversation centred upon hunting, and the Earl had seized on the subject as enthusiastically as his brother.

Ann consoled herself at this point with the reflection that at least neither Lord Branthorpe nor his quiet, soft-eyed friend had shown the least inclination to get foxed as she had feared. As for Lady Amelia and Ralph Lambert she had scarcely had time to notice them, although all the eyes of the assembled company had been on Ralph when he arrived in claret velvet tailcoat, gray nankin pantaloons and flowing cravat.

Now, telling herself firmly that John was the only person who really mattered to her at the gathering, Ann murmured excuses in her mother's unheeding ear and set off to find him. Before she could do so the late arrival of the Winthorpe party was announced and she hurried to greet them. Mr. and Mrs. James Winthorpe and their two daughters had brought an extra guest with them, and Ann barely had time to catch the name "Miss Clarissa Merivale" before that lady was excitably demanding to see Lord Branthorpe. As Ann escorted the unexpected guest in search of the Earl, John's description "a red-headed light-skirt" came unaccountably into her mind.

*   *   *

Simon drew back into the corner of the coach and brushed the snowflakes from his evening cloak. "By Jupiter, it strikes cold after the Dorville's over-heated drawing-room, doesn't it?" he said.

Amelia agreed, teeth chattering, and John scuffed the snow off his thin dancing shoes and complained that he would have brought his riding boots if he'd known it would snow again. Surprisingly, only Philip seemed to be still in in a rosy glow from the evening's exertions.

"It's lucky we ordered the coach for 11 o'clock—it's snowing hard now," Amelia commented, as the flakes began to cling to the windows.

Simon reflected it had been *very* lucky for him that they had arranged to leave early due to their state of mourning for Clarissa's totally unexpected appearance had quite ruined the entertainment for him. She had traced him, so she maintained, by casually mentioning his name to her uncle, James Winthorpe, who just happened to be in Town, and she had also seen the *Gazette* announcement of Simon's father's death. It was enough for Simon that she had spoiled his evening although, latterly, she had transferred her attentions to John: Simon wondered if he had recognised her.

It had been an evening of surprises and not all pleasant by any means. Even before they had arrived at Shipton Grange he had discovered that Amelia, too, was making her first social appearance that evening since her return home almost a year before. Simon had evidently shown his surprise and before he could question his sister further, John had interrupted.

Simon's reaction to being received at the Grange by Miss Dorville and her father had turned from delight on recognising the Vision seen at the Swan, to instantaneous chagrin as he realised she was John's fiancée. How could he have guessed from his brother's description of her? he reflected ruefully. John's assessment of Mrs. Dorville, however, had proved accurate in one respect; she had indeed toad eaten Simon from the moment he appeared, but John need have had no qualms that she would advert to their earlier, less fortunate meeting which the squire had so enjoyed. Simon had seen Squire Wharton watching their second encounter closely, and that gentleman had been disappointed by his hostess's evident lack of reaction. He was compensated fully at dinner though, when he witnessed Mrs.

Dorville eating the *escargot pâté*. Simon smiled to himself in the darkness of the coach: it would not surprise
him if Jules had served those snails for the very purpose of upsetting Mrs. Dorville, for the dish was obviously not of her choosing! Simon was sorry, in that
event, that the chef had not been able to see the lady
as realisation had spread across her large, haughty features.

The occupants of the slow-moving coach were
silent: both John and Philip had closed their eyes and
Amelia was staring thoughtfully across at Philip. Simon
noticed his friend looked rather flushed and tired but
hazarded that he had enjoyed the rout; he danced
several times and once with Amelia. A picture of the
Byronic-looking Ralph Lambert suddenly came into his
mind and he realised that he had learned nothing during the course of the evening of his sister's relationship
with the boy. Mr. Lambert had disdained both dancing
and cards as occupations and had spent a considerable
part of his time questioning Simon about India; not, as
he explained, that he had any intention of going there,
but he needed the material for an epic poem of tiger-
hunting. He had not seemed particularly attentive to
Amelia but then, Simon thought gloomily, he would
have been careful to avoid singling her out in the circumstances. They had sat together at dinner, of course,
so perhaps Miss Dorville had had some reason for the
placing?

The coach suddenly jolted to a halt, and John,
roused by the shouts of the coachman, reluctantly
opened the door and jumped down.

"It's not much—horse down, that's all. Slipped in
the snow, I expected," he informed the shivering in-
mates of the coach. He shut the door at last and went
to help.

It seemed an age before he returned, and Simon

hoped he would not have to get out too. He was thoroughly chilled and feared a return of his fever. In less than ten minutes, in fact, they were on their way again and this time the journey was completed safely.

THIRTEEN

THE EARL of Branthorpe woke early next morning, and was rather surprised to find he felt quite well. He had been glad for once of Joliffe's fussy insistence that a warming pan be run over the linen sheets, for he had been thoroughly chilled by their delayed journey home the night before—short though it was.

Later, at breakfast, he was tackling his second slice of home-cured ham when his brother joined him. John had surprised him over the port the previous night by displaying a great deal of knowledge of Lord Wellington's recent lack of progress in Spain, and by his close interest in the Peninsula campaigns.

"You have no thick head this morning, I collect," John commented, eyeing Simon's plate.

"Naturally not, I am known for my abstemious ways!" his lordship said as primly as was possible with a mouthful of ham.

John laughed. "All right, you have made your point.

Your character has been much maligned, and I've said I'm sorry."

From this generous response, Simon had to assume that his brother had not associated Miss Merivale with his unfortunate appearance outside the London hotel.

"I thoroughly enjoyed myself last night," his lordship said, politely if not with complete truth. "You're a lucky devil you know."

John came back from the side table with a laden plate, and sat beside his brother. "Ann, you mean," he replied casually. "Oh yes, but I was damned glad there was no formal announcement of our engagement. Mrs. Dorville had been pressing for it, I know, but I can't abide a lot of fuss."

"No, but I'll warrant it was scarcely necessary anyway. You took Ann into dinner, and were seen to stand up with her several times. That will be taken as sufficient evidence of an attachment, by the local populace, I'll wager!" Simon pointed out.

"I suppose you are right," John agreed. "I say, I'm glad you introduced me to Miss Merivale," he added, with a sudden enthusiasm.

His lordship's coffee cup checked in mid-air, and he cast a wary glance at his brother. "Ah yes, Miss Merivale!" he repeated in hearty but vague tones, hoping for further enlightenment.

"Well, I've wanted to meet James Winthorpe for an age! He's got a terrific string of hunting nags, you know," John volunteered.

"No, I had no idea," murmured Simon carefully.

"Oh yes, and Miss Merivale insisted he invite me over to see his stables whenever I wish."

"Splendid," remarked Simon. "You are thinking of buying something from him?" he asked tentatively.

John gave a sheepish grin. "Oh well, you never know. Later on perhaps. But I did think he may be interested in some of yours as they are soon to be in the market," he suggested, and with surprisingly little rancour in the circumstances, Simon thought.

"I will bear him in mind certainly," his lordship said, pleased. "John, I am persuaded this is as good a moment as any to tell you—it is my intention that you and your future wife shall have two of those hunters as a wedding gift."

John looked embarrassed. "Oh—thank you, that's very generous," he mumbled to his plate.

"Devil a bit! I wish you could keep the lot, believe me, but if this estate can't run to their upkeep at present, I'm sure Wragston won't for a time yet."

John looked thoughtful. "I suppose you're right, but remember my pockets won't be to let exactly, when I'm married."

"Far from it, judging by the Settlement, but, well, I don't want to read you a lecture—"

"Oh no!" retorted John cynically, "I'm sure you don't."

Simon persisted. "I had an interesting talk with Dorville last night—I liked him, I must say—and he's worked damned hard for his money, you know. And, more than anything else, I think he'd like to see his grandchildren benefit a bit from that." He looked earnestly at his brother, who was busy checking the level of the coffee left in the pot. "Don't spend it *all* on horses, John, that's all I'll say." Simon was uncomfortably aware that his motive for saying this had very little to do with Dorville. It was the daughter he was trying to safeguard, for he had a feeling that John wasn't the right husband for her; and it was too late now to alter that.

"Grandchildren!" John cried, startled, and momentarily stopped refilling Simon's coffee cup. "Oh yes," he acknowledged truculently a slight flush staining his fair complexion, "but it's going to be uncommonly dull at Wragston, I can tell you. I shall have to keep the stables up to have something to do."

Simon was spared the task of gratuitously pointing out to his young brother that setting up a house with a delightful wife, and managing an estate as run-down as Wragston was, should prove anything but dull, by the arrival of Amelia.

"Oh, I thought I should be the first down this morning," she said, ringing for some more coffee.

"Good Lord, no!" retorted John, leaning back in his chair and yawning cavernously. "We've been up for hours haven't we, Simon? But I must be off to the stables now, to check if that wheeler is lame after its fall last night," he said, suddenly brisk.

"He seems in a very good mood today," commented Amelia when John had left them.

"Yes, and believe it or not, it appears we have Miss Merivale to thank for it," Simon told her, laughing.

His sister's fair brows were drawn together in puzzlement until Simon explained about the Winthorpes. "Mind you," he went on, "it doesn't seem to have occurred to him that he would have met them anyway last night, with or without Miss Merivale—or me."

"What did he think of her?" asked Amelia.

"Do you know, I don't recall he expressed any opinion, one way or the other," Simon replied, much struck.

"I do hope that's not a sinister sign, then," Amelia said pensively, buttering a piece of French bread. "I did wonder at the time," she added obscurely.

"Sinister?" echoed Simon. "What are you talking about?"

"John's *penchant* for mature ladies," she told him succinctly. "You may not have heard about it."

"Well, really—" his lordship started to say, then recalling Joliffe's remarks on the subject, considered for a moment. "No, I'm sure you must be wrong."

"Oh no, he definitely finds them irresistible," Amelia said categorically.

"No, Melly, I mean you're wrong about Miss Merivale."

"Well, there's no accounting for taste on that head, is there?" she commented sharply. "And, anyway, I didn't consider she looked so repellent."

Beginning to feel a shade ill-at-ease at the turn the conversation had taken, Simon asked if she had enjoyed her evening.

"Oh yes, I did!" Then, after a brief pause, she said: "But how one's neighbours have changed in a few short years. You must have thought so yourself."

"The Wharton boys, you mean?" Simon asked, cautiously avoiding mention of Ralph Lambert, the obvious candidate for comment.

"Oh yes, I suppose they've changed, but only as one would expect. No, I meant Mr. Lambert, I nearly went into whoops when I saw him! He was used to be such a dull, prosaic-looking boy—but always handsome, I suppose," she admitted in a detached manner, and took a sip of the hot coffee just provided by Stagg.

This was Simon's second surprise during the course of breakfast, and for a moment he could only stare. "Mrs. Wharton led me to understand such attire is all the crack with some—young men," he said faintly, playing for time again.

"Yes, but it was sadly out of place at a country rout," said Amelia critically. "I can't think why he accepted the invitation at all."

The butler was hovering by the table.

"That will be all, Stagg," Simon told him, as he resolved to pursue this Lambert affair to the end with Amelia.

"Yes, m'lord, but before I go," the butler said firmly, "Mr. Trant sends his regrets, and will not be down for breakfast this morning."

"Oh? What's amiss, do you know, Stagg?" his lordship enquired.

"Only that he is far from being up to snuff, as Mr. Joliffe termed it," the butler repeated with distaste.

"Thank you, Stagg," said Simon dismissively, a worried crease between his dark brows.

"He didn't indulge too freely in the port last night, did he, Simon?" asked Amelia.

"No, Phil's fond of his food, I'll not deny, but very sparing with the drink—even when tempted with Dorville's excellent cellar."

"I sat opposite him at dinner, and I don't think he ate very much either."

"Did he not?" commented Simon quickly. "Well, I'd best go up to him."

"I'll wait here. Come back and let me know what's wrong, won't you?" Amelia asked him anxiously.

"Of course," her brother assured her, vaguely aware that something rather important had slipped his mind since hearing of Philip's indisposition.

Joliffe intercepted his master outside Mr. Trant's bedchamber door. "Ah, I'm glad to see you, my lord. You'll know what's best to be done, I dare say."

"What is it?" Simon said urgently, knowing the valet to be capable of coping with most contingencies unaided.

"Fever, my lord, but I've not seen its like before."

"I'll wager I have," replied Simon, grim-faced, when he heard the details. "It will be a return of his Indian fever, confound it!"

"Is it serious?" asked the valet.

"Not usually fatal, if that's what you mean, but it is not to be supposed that getting thoroughly chilled last night will have helped matters. Come, we'll go in and see him. If it is as I fear, we will need to get a dose of bark into him without delay."

Philip was pale and very restless—the bedclothes being in a turmoil, although it was scarcely two minutes since Joliffe said, he had left them all right and tight.

"Simon," said Philip in roughened tones, "so sorry about this. It's my damnable fever again. I hoped I'd seen the last of it. I've no wish to impose upon you—is the weather improved?" he concluded, hoarse and anxious.

Simon saw that his brown eyes were unnaturally bright and he was shivering violently, but he was still in possession of his faculties at least. "Don't you fret about that, Phil. You'll stay here as long as need be." He asked Joliffe to find Mr. Trant's medicine chest, and was glad now that his friend's mother had insisted on packing it so carefully in Lyme. "We'll have you right as a trivet in no time. You pulled me through mine in much worse circumstances than these, remember?" Simon said bracingly.

Joliffe, who was placing the polished wooden box on the night-table, heard these words and looked sharply at his master. "You've had this fever, my lord?"

"Not this recurrent one, so don't get in a pucker over that! This is quite a mild distemper," he explained in a confused effort to hearten both his hearers.

However, Joliffe did not look convinced, and Philip seemed to take no marked interest in the exchange. The valet poured out a measure of the bark into a glass, and it was administered to the patient who pulled a long face at its acrid taste.

Simon smiled at his friend smypathetically. "I know, Phil, abominable isn't it?" He turned to the valet. "Go down to the kitchen to see Jules. I'll warrant he's got some appetising broth brewing down there; if not, a posset will serve. Oh—and have hot bricks sent up, too."

For once, Philip said he did not think he could swallow another thing. While Joliffe was absent, Simon tried to distract his friend by telling him of John's cheerful acceptance of Clarissa Merivale. Then Philip asked about Amelia, and this immediately put his lordship in remembrance of his resolve to question her about Lambert; so, when the valet returned, he went promptly back to the breakfast parlour.

The table had been cleared, and Amelia was standing by the window looking out through the leaded panes at the wintry parkland. She turned on hearing Simon come in.

"Is it thawing yet, do you think?" he asked casually, as he joined her.

"It may be. Why? Is a doctor needed urgently?" she asked, frowning.

"No, I think we'll call no doctors at this stage. We still rely on old Jackson from York, I collect? Yes, well, I doubt his knowledge of tropical disorders is extensive, and his universal remedy of bleeding can be treid later if Philip does not respond—which I am sure he will," he added hastily.

"Tropical?" echoed Amelia, looking at her brother wide-eyed. "He has a fever? Is it so hopeless then, that a doctor is unnecessary?" she asked, disregarding his assurances.

"No, of course not, Melly. Don't put yourself about. This is a simple fever, which he's had before, and I know how to treat it. I've seen it many times, and as like as not he'll be over it in four-and-twenty hours."

"How can you be sure? He's been thoroughly chilled lately—on Friday when you went to York, and again last night, you know."

"Well, I am sure," affirmed Simon, who was worried and trying hard not to lose his temper. "It's not like you to be thrown into a quake by sickness."

She looked a little guilty, and said abruptly: "I'm sorry."

"You must believe me, I shan't let anything happen to Phil if it is in my power to prevent it," her brother assured her.

Amelia was wearing a fine gray merino gown, with a high ruched neck, and over it her red shawl. Nursing one elbow, she restlessly twisted the locket with her other hand. "Here's the boy coming down the drive with the letters," she said.

"Well, you don't sound very pleased about it," commented her brother, smiling.

"Mm? Oh, I'm not waiting for any letters," she replied vaguely.

Simon decided to broach the subject which was worrying him. "Melly, earlier, when we were talking about the rout last night, you seemed to be very critical of Ralph Lambert."

She stared blankly at him. "Yes, well what has that to say to anything. He wasn't a particular friend of yours, was he?"

"Well, no," her brother said, baffled. "But I thought him to be a friend of yours."

It was Amelia's turn to look bewildered. "Mine! Oh Simon, you must still have a poor opinion of my taste! How could you?" she said, and laughed at him.

"What else would you have me think, after all those surreptitious visits to Kerswell?" he retorted crossly.

She put a hand to her mouth, and the laughter ceased. "Oh no, pray don't ask me about that again, I beg you."

"Look, I don't know what sort of a rig you and mama are running between you, but I can tell you this much, she intends it to cease very shortly." Simon was incensed now by the secrecy, and spoke sharper than he intended; he instantly regretted this.

Amelia turned a white face to him. "Did mama say anything more to you?" she enquired in a scarcely audible whisper.

"How could she, when I'm to be kept in the dark until everything is settled?" Her expression caused him to moderate his tone. "Melly, you *must* share this. I may be able to help," he pleaded.

It seemed a great effort for her to speak at all. "All right, I will tell you, but only because I know you can't do anything—no-one can," she said tonelessly.

"Come, sit down," recommended her brother, gently.

"No, I beg you don't sympathise with me or I shall not be able to continue." She took a deep breath. "I have not been visiting Kerswell, as you think, but one of the gamekeeper's cottages on their estate. My daughter is there, you see—"

"Good lord," murmured Simon.

"—and the gamekeeper's wife is acting as wet nurse," Amelia went on.

"Then why all the hugger-mugger, for heaven's sake?" her brother demanded. "By Jupiter, I'm an uncle!" he added, much struck.

"Simon, it's not as simple as that," Amelia cried desperately. "It is not to be supposed I can raise a bastard child here! I was never married you know."

Her brother felt this to be an accusation, and he realised his foolishness had been responsible for more even than he had feared. "But does anyone know you are other than a widow?" he argued.

"Papa certainly knew," she flung at him, "and he stipulated I could remain here only if I consented to the child being adopted."

"That was monstrous, certainly, but I expect he would have come about if he'd lived," Simon hazarded, but without much conviction.

"Well, he showed no sign of doing so, and the child was well over six months old when he died," she retorted.

"Then she must be nigh on eight months now," Simon calculated. "and I deem it high time she was brought back here. I don't like a niece of mine treated so," he said lightly. "She must be dark, indeed, if that is her hair which you have in your locket," he added as an after-thought.

"Yes it is," Amelia snapped. "But stop funning! I've made up my mind about this; it hasn't been easy, and I told you I don't want any interference this time."

"All right," her brother sighed. "You're quite right to lay the blame at my door, but I do think you're storing up a lot of unnecessary misery for yourself this way."

"Mama says it would blight my future chances of marriage completely, and she's quite right. I couldn't marry and not tell my husband the truth—and it's not a very pretty story is it? Frederick was quite notorious, you know, and I can't see his child being accepted willingly by anyone."

Simon suspected she was relieved to be telling him about this, and he risked questioning her a little further. "When did you discover you were not legally wed, Melly?"

She stared out of the window, a set expression on her face. "Oh, I was as stupid as you over that!" she exclaimed bitterly. "Frederick told me when he heard I was pregnant. I was pressing him to find us more suitable lodgings. but he lost his temper and disclaimed his legal responsibility in the matter."

Her brother was appalled. "But why didn't you leave

him right away, and come home then?" he asked tentatively.

"Because I am persuaded papa would have shown me the door. Anyway, I always hoped Frederick might change, I suppose. He did say he would try to find somewhere better for us. I was sorry for him in a way, and I did love him at first," Amelia said, almost to herself. "There was no real malice in him, but he was weak. He had been cheated at the gaming tables and in desperation had taken out post obits, which he had no hope of redeeming. His only answer was to rely more and more on gaming to recruit."

Simon reflected that none of this suggested that a child of Frederick's would bear any particular taint; seemed to have been no worse than many in suffering from the widespread mania for gambling. However, he forebore to say this, as he felt that Amelia was merely repeating excuses, and did not really believe all she said on the matter herself. "I think you would find, you know, that if someone really loved you, the child would not be any obstacle," Simon submitted carefully.

"No," responded Amelia coldly. "I thought that at first, but I know now I would rather be unencumbered. Oh, it may sound heartless to you, but I would like to make a fresh start, and this is the only way. It will not be easy for me to ensnare a husband now, in any event," she stared bitterly. Then, after a pause, she added: "You must never discuss this with anyone—not a soul. And that includes mama, Simon. Remember she that he was not an ideal parent was obvious, but he is only carrying out papa's wishes in the matter," she cautioned him.

Simon had initially been quite astounded by his sister's disclosure, and, beyond an instinctive feeling that she should keep the child, he had not thought further, but now an idea flashed though his mind. "Melly! How would it be if I claimed the child as my own? A little drawback brought home from India. Such behaviour in a man would not be considered in the least remarkable, and I am doubtless thought to be beyond the pale in any event."

Amelia looked at her brother as though she did not know whether to laugh or cry. "Oh, Simon, she may be darkhaired, but she's not dark-skinned, too!" she said in a choking voice.

Simon was affronted. "Well, really, that's the outside of enough!"

"How so? You cast aspersions on my taste in partners, as I recall, at the outset of this discussion," she pointed out primly.

"*Touché,* but there is a difference, if I may say so. All the same, you should take my proposals seriously, I think. Consider, I could say instead I had married out there, if you like. My wife died in childbrith—and there is nothing out of the way in that, a terrible number of Englishwomen do in India. Philip's wife did," he interpolated. "Then I brought the child back here to safeguard its life. Now, had your child been a boy it might have presented problems of inheritance, and so forth. But, don't you see, Melly, it would not be in any degree out of the way for me to bring in a nurse here with the child. And when they were here, it would be all of a piece that you should take charge."

"That's all very fine whilst we are both at home," said Amelia, evidently interested in her brother's scheme in spite of herself. "But what happens when you marry? Your wife would be expected to take the child then."

"But I've not the smallest intention of marrving," declared Simon, and, although he was almost surprised to hear himself say this, he meant it. "John's marriage will remove any necessity from me to produce an heir."

"Even so—and I don't believe you for one moment—you can hardly be proposing that *my* future husband should take over *your* daughter. Why I had as lief ask him to accept my own illegitimate child; it would be less bizarre. No, Simon," she said, sounding very weary, "it won't fadge, you know."

Simon frowned, and bit his lip. "I own I had not thought of that contingency. But there must be some way out of this!" he cried. "After all, this is my roof and I don't object to your child living here. Mama would soon get used to it, I dare say."

"No, I beg you. This time I don't want your help. Oh, I know you mean it for the best, and I do appreciate it." She smiled uncertainly at him, but he saw her eyes were filled with tears; she turned away quickly. "You said, Mr. Trant's wife died in childbirth. What happened to the child?" she asked in a strangled voice.

"Mm? Oh, it died of fever, too, a few days later, I believe."

"Poor Mr. Trant. I am better off than he," Amelia whispered, then she abruptly spun on her heel and went to the door. "Let me know how he is, soon, won't you?" she pleaded, and left her brother to his confused thoughts.

FOURTEEN

SHORTLY AFTER his sister had left the breakfast parlour, the Earl followed suit and went to look in on Philip, whose fever was now beginning to mount. But as this was only to be expected, his lordship was not unduly concerned; Joliffe was doing everything that was necessary for Mr. Trant's comfort.

Simon decided to gallop some of the ebullience out of the mettlesome Sinner and hoped, at the same time, to clear his own head and see an acceptable way out of his sister's formidable tangle. The one thing he did not want at the moment was to have any private converse with his mother until he was quite sure of his own attitude.

He was in the stables tightening the girths on Sinner, a task which the stable lads did not relish, when Matt put his grizzled head over the stall door. "Her ladyship's calling for you, seemingly, m'lord," he informed his master.

"Dammit," Simon muttered under his breath, then made a quick decision. "I've left, Matt, not a moment ago, there's a good fellow." He hazarded the old groom would enjoy being party to this minor deception, and it seemed he was not out in his reckoning, for the old boy said: "Ay, m'lord," in a hoarse whisper, and went off cackling to himself. Simon hastily removed the head-stall, put the bridle on, and led the lively gray sorrel out of the back of the stables.

At the end of an hour, a temporarily subdued Sinner was back in his stall, and his rider, also looking sub-died and thoughtful, was walking back to the house. The meeting with his mother could not be long delayed, and as soon as Simon had changed his boots he sought her out. There was, as far as he had been able to determine, only one course open to Amelia, but it would need the co-operation of two people, and time, not all of which would be necessarily forthcoming, he feared. It also entailed what could only be described—by even the most charitable—as meddling, and he did not relish the prospect open before him.

The Dowager kept to her room in the morning, but not to lie idly abed; she was seated at a small bureau when her eldest son knocked and went in.

"Good morning, mama, you wished to see me, I collect?"

"I do," she acknowledged briskly, "On a matter which is important but not desperately urgent, fortunately." Then, in a different tone of voice, she contin-ued: "Mr. Trant is not well, I understand."

"No, I very much regret he is not. It looks as though he is in for a bad bout of fever," Simon told her.

"I'm exceedingly sorry to hear it. I own to having a kindness for him." She looked severely at her son. "I would as lief have heard of his sickness other than from my maid Ellis, but no matter."

Her son reflected that he was being made to feel at a disadvantage before their discussion, whatever it may be, and he wished she would come to the point. He had determined to honour Amelia's wishes, and not reveal that he knew about the child's existence to his mother, but it was not easy. With one glossy boot-clad foot resting on the equally burnished brass fender, he picked up a *Sèvres* figure of a shepherdess, and remembered, for some inexplicable reason, how he had thought it a likeness of Amelia when he was a boy. It did not resemble her remotely; he could see that now. He smiled to himself.

"Do you stop fidgeting, Simon," recommended the Dowager irritably.

Simon replaced the ornament carefully, and realised from his mother's exeptional reproof that she was disturbed over something. Then he noticed there was a letter in her hand.

"I heard from your Aunt Lennox this morning," the Dowager said at last.

"Oh yes," her son returned in a non-committal voice, hoping, uncharitably, that this formidable dame was not proposing to honour them with a visit. However, he thought she would be well able to contain her transports, even if she had just learned of his return to the family home.

"I do not scruple to tell you that I had far rather not have to involve you in this matter at all. In truth, I vowed I would not. But there, it seems I have no choice."

Simon was impatient with this preamble, but also hopeful that it might, at last, concern his sister. After all, she had been watching the arrival of the letters that morning, with an air of foreboding.

"When Aunt Lennox came here for your father's funeral, I had a long talk with her, Simon, and found her so sympathetic and full of good sense that I told her of Amelia's plight."

"What! Aunt Lennox sympathetic!" exclaimed Simon, unwisely startled into speech which hindered the narrative.

The Dowager was slowly folding and re-folding the letter. "Oh, yes, beneath the blunt exterior there is a great understanding. In short," she went on, with seeming reluctance, "she offered her good offices in the matter, and this is the result." She held up the crumpled missive.

Simon, who was still supposed to be in the dark over the entire affair, waited cautiously for her to explain, although he was delighted that he was evidently to be taken into her confidence at last.

"I deeply regret having had to mislead you over your sister, but I hoped to conclude matters on my own. You must have suspected all manner of *mésalliances,* but the truth is quite simple—she had a child about three months after she returned ho—"

"Good God!" cried Simon, and hoped he sounded suitably surprised.

"There is no call to sound quite so dismayed," remonstrated his mother mildly. "It is not a totally unheard of occurrence, you know. However, Aunt Lennox tells me she has discovered some eminently suitable parents in Derbyshire, where the child may be fixed. It will all be accomplished in the most discreet manner, and Amelia need have no knowledge of their identity or whereabouts. The only problem remaining is how to remove the child from the cottage on the Kerswell estate—I'm surprised you haven't asked what happened to the child," she interposed, "—and with the minimum number of people involved. The baby will be in Betsy's care on the journey into Derbyshire, for it is her sister who is nursing the child at present, and you will drive them there—"

Simon felt it was high time to intervene at this point. "And if I refuse?"

"I hope you will nto do anything so ill-judged, but if you should, I shall be compelled to ask John. It will need a close-carriage and no groom will be permissible. I own I place infinitely more trust in your ability to accomplish the journey without over-setting the coach or otherwise causing a commotion, than I do in your brother's."

"Mama, surely the servants are well aware of the present situation already?" her son argued, avoiding the main issue for the moment.

"I am sure they are not," stated the Dowager unequivocally. "I paid a great deal of money for the presence of a man-midwife from London at the birth and, when he left, the child was taken by Betsy to her sister to be wet-nursed. The sister had given birth to her own child only a month before, and the two have been raised together. Betsy, of course, is utterly trustworthy, and her sister, being a gamekeeper's wife, lives in the most isolated manner."

"It all sounds exceedingly Gothic, if I may say so," remarked Simon distastefully. "It was made known to the servants in due course that the child had perished, I collect?"

"It was. And Amelia's lowness of spirits served to corroborate the fact," sighed the Dowager.

"This is beyond everything, ma'am! Really, I cannot give my hand to any part of your stratagems. And if John had an ounce of sensibility, nor would he!" He paused. "What would you have done had Betsy not been blessed with such an eligible sister?" he asked curtly.

The Dowager was unruffled. "In some ways it would have rendered my distasteful task easier. The child would have been sent to a more distant nurse, and one unconnected with this household. As it was, Amelia quite cleverly suggested it would be thought fitting in her to visit Betsy's sister, to show there was no ill-will over the unfortunate death of her baby." The Dowager smiled ruefully. "From that moment, of course, I had difficulty in keeping her away from the cottage."

Simon pursued another course. "I cannot like Aunt Lennox being used in this manner, either. Her son admittedly, was of the greatest service to me when I went to India, but we should not resort constantly to their help in concealing our dirty linen!"

"Fiddlesticks! I do not see the matter in such a sordid light. It is essential Amelia should have a fresh start and, this way, a couple who have long wanted a daughter will be rendered happy—"

Simon interrupted anxiously. "Just how far have the arrangements advanced? Are the couple in daily expectation of the child's arrival?"

"Oh no. Aunt Lennox is quite specific on that point—she has simply made very discreet and tentative enquiries to ascertain their willingess to take a child into their home."

"Thank God for that, at least!" exclaimed Simon, in an unguarded moment.

The Dowager fixed him with a severe eye. "And what am I to understand from that remark?" she asked.

Her son moved away from the hearth impatiently. "Anything you wish, ma'am, but I need time to think this over," he said in irate tones. "For the moment you will do nothing further in this affair."

"I'll not tolerate your distressing Amelia afresh," the Dowager cautioned. "I am persuaded she had resigned herself to this outcome now."

"Mama, believe me, my sole desire in this is to mitigate the long term consequences on my sister," Simon said in a kindlier tone. "I may not be able to do anything, but I would like a little time in which to try."

The Dowager gave an odd little smile, and placed the letter in a pigeon-hole of the bureau. "Very well, Simon. A few more days will not signify, I dare say, and in any event I think you should stay here until Mr. Trant shows an improvement," she conceded.

Simon wished he had put forward that reason himself earlier, for that way he could have avoided remonstrating with his mother. "Thank you, ma'am, and I apologise for speaking sharply. I own this has been a rather disconcerting morning," he said with all honesty. A thought suddenly occurred to him, and he hesitated, his hand on the door know. "Why is it Joliffe has never made mention of this to me, in even the most fleeting manner, I wonder?"

"Because I warned him not to, for fear of distressing you. Knowing the circumstances of the case, he quite understood that the child's death should not be mentioned. I know him to be an inverterate gossip, and the only servant liable to broach the subject with you."

Simon drew in a deep breath. "You certainly appear to have thought of every contingency, ma'am."

"I hope I have," his mother returned trenchantly.

After her son had gone, the Dowager rose rather stiffly from the desk and stood before the fire for a time, hands outstretched to the flames. All in all, she was not sorry to have shared this burden finally with her son, and considered the interview had gone tolerably well.

*　　*　　*

His lordship repaired to the book-room before luncheon to write a letter. As he folded and wafered it, then wrote his name across the bottom left-hand corner, he was grateful for his good fortune in being able, now, to frank his own letters. This privilege meant also that he had a check on all mail leaving the house. He was sure his mother would not communicate with Aunt Lennox now, but he would know if she did.

Luncheon was inevitably a gloomy and rather tense affair, enlivened only by John's announcement that he had called upon his fiancée that morning, and discovered that an ailing Miss Merivale had stayed there overnight. "I thought I should call, as I hazarded there would be a few guests stranded by the snow. I'm glad I did, too, for I can be of some service in conveying Miss Merivale home tomorrow."

Amelia, who was eating very little, and saying less, exchanged a swift glance with Simon.

"It depends on whether she is quite recovered by then, of course," John added.

"She had contracted nothing of a serious nature, I hope?" his sister asked, to spare Simon showing any particular concern for the lady.

"Just the headache, I understand. She gets 'em every now and then," John responded casually. "But it's a splendid chance for me to go down to Little Sutton, eh, Simon?"

"Oh, yes," agreed his brother absent-mindedly, whilst trying to recall if Miss Merivale had always had a susceptibility to headaches, but he remembered her as being exceedingly hardy, even in the Indian climate. It made him uneasy to think of her so close at hand. "Yes, I think it's a famous notion, John," Simon affirmed more enthusiastically. "Why not rack up there for the night, if you can?" he suggested, in the hope of removing his brother from his mother's reach for a time, should she decide to call for his assistance after all.

The interference did not escape the Dowager, and she gave Simon a sardonic look.

His lordship feared he had overplayed his hand, for

it was not, when all was said and done, a great distance to travel, but John took to the idea at once.

"Of course!" he exclaimed, "and I can collect my new riding boots from York on the way back. They weren't ready when I looked in on Saturday." He looked round the table. "If anyone wants anything from York I'll be happy to oblige," he offered.

There was no response and, if John noticed his family were exceptionally downcast, he no doubt related it to Mr. Trant's illness, and gave it no further thought.

For the rest of the day Simon spent much of his time with his friend, who had passed painfully, now, into fevered restlessness after an ague which had racked his frame until his very teeth seemed to rattle like dice. As Simon devoted all his attention to Philip's welfare, he endeavoured to set aside all other problems until such time as his friend should show some improvement.

FIFTEEN

NO MESSAGE was received at Branthorpe the following morning from Shipton Grange, so John assumed that Miss Merivale was sufficiently recovered to undertake the journey home. He left, about two o'clock, in the curricle and with a groom up behind. In marked contrast with the rest of the household, he seemed in better spirits than usual.

From Philip's bedchamber window, Simon watched as the carriage splashed through the slushy drive and away to the main lodge gates, cutting dark, deep ruts as it went.

Joliffe had spent the night on a truckle bed in Mr. Trant's room and, as far as his lordship could ascertain, had had little sleep. Simon had found his friend to be delirious in the morning, and only now was he beginning to show signs of falling into a natural sleep. The valet, after a morning's rest, was due to return to the sick-room soon, and Simon decided to ride out again for an hour.

Sinner was no less restive than the day before, and just to show he was unimpressed by his master's overdue attentions, he aimed a spiteful kick at Simon while he was taking the bridle down from a wall hook.

"Oh, you would, you, you old varmint?" cried his lordship, springing lightly out of the way. "I'll put you through your paces for that," he promised the gray.

Simon was glad to have something straightforward and active to occupy him, and during the next hour he covered a good many miles of the estate. The difficulty was that he was out of practise and Sinner knew this well: he had twice tried to throw his rider and had come nearer to success than was good for Simon's dignity. There was a very difficult hedge in his way home, and he determined to put Sinner to it to show him who was master. The sorrel took it with deceptive meekness until the very last moment when he seemed about to refuse. Simon would not consent to be balked in this manner; he gripped mightily with his knees, and refraining from startling the beast with his whip, got him over by will-power alone. It was exceedingly wet at the far side of the hedge with rapidly thawing snow, and Sinner contrived to kick up an unconscionable amount of mud on to his rider's boots and buckskins as a final indignity.

"Well done, my lord!" cried a feminine voice close by.

Simon looked to his right and saw Miss Dorville cantering towards him. "I felt a mere tyro, I confess ma'am," he laughed. "I was within a whisker of being pitched between the brute's ears!"

"Well, that's a fate your brother has experienced more than once on Sinner, I fear," Miss Dorville told her neighbour.

"Really!" exclaimed his lordship, surprised. "I had no notion he had ventured near the beast."

Ann had drawn her own mount level with Sinner, but at a respectful distance. "I should not have adverted to the matter then! John would never forgive me," she said, repentant.

"Rest assured, *I* shall not be the one to tax him on the subject," returned his lordship sardonically, whilst thinking to himself that Miss Dorville would look more at home in Hyde Park than in a muddy Yorkshire field. Her blue riding habit, with black frogging, and a black beaver hat decorated with a blue ostrich feather curling in a jaunty manner against her cheek, made him feel quite unkempt beside such elegance, and Sinner hadn't helped.

"I must apologise for trespassing, but I have grown accustomed to stealing into your fields to exercise my bay," Ann said a little wearily—or so it seemed to her companion.

"Then I hope very much you will continue to do so, although I own it seems improbable you should steal anywhere in that magnificent habit. Shall we ride on?" he suggested, fearing that Sinner would soon seek to terrorise Miss Dorville's much smaller mount, and he had no wish to explain to an incensed John that his fiancée had been unseated. "I hope my brother has not presented a despotic picture of me, Miss Dorville?" he said quizzically.

"Oh no, not in the least," she responded smoothly. "In fact he has spoken of you very little."

He thought he detected a twinkle in those wonderful blue eyes. "Ah, I see, that sets me very roundly in my place," he said wryly. "I should have asked before, but I trust Miss Merivale made a complete recovery?"

Ann looked guardedly at her companion. "Indeed yes. She seemed quite stout again this morning," she said, in a voice which lacked warmth.

No doubt about it the twinkle had quite vanished now, he thought. However, it would not be the thing to speak ill of Clarissa if John was about to strike up a cordial acquaintance with the lady, and he cursed her coming yet again. "It seems she had carried my brother away," he commented, and wondered how Miss Dorville viewed the fact.

Ann found herself justifying John's action, thinking her companion to be jealous of him.

"Yes, it relieved papa of the duty, and I own I anticipated John would be living in the pockets of the Winthorpe family once he discovered their mutual interest!"

"We all had a most enjoyable time the other night, and I would like to thank you for re-introducing me to my neighbours in such a pleasurable manner," Simon told her gratefully, hoping Clarissa would be forgotten for a while.

"Oh, you must think me the most dreadful ingrate!" Ann exclaimed. "I have not thanked you for your gift. It is the most charming print," she said politely.

"If you liked it, I believe there is a whole series. I

hope I may have the opportunity to present you with them all in the future."

"Thank you, you are very kind," murmured Ann, but her face was momentarily obscured as she brushed a straying lock of dark hair aside with her gloved hand.

"Did my brother tell you of our guest's sudden illness?" Simon asked her.

Ann gave him an anxious look. "No. Mr. Trant you mean?"

"Yes, but I merely wished to reassure you that his sickness has no possible connection with the revelries on Saturday. It is a fever he brought back from India. We were there together."

"Well, I do hope he recovers soon," Ann said kindly, then seemed about to say more but hesitated and was silent.

His lordship, surmising that she was curious about him, said: "I had a much more severe bout myself just before I sailed for home. It accounts for my dark, lean and dissolute aspect—which has drawn much unfavourable comment upon me, I may say!" he concluded with amusement.

"Oh, but I believe a dark complexion is all the rage amongst the dandy set! They dye their cheeks with walnut juice, I have heard, to achieve just such an effect," she retorted, with dancing eyes.

"I am obliged to you for that comforting intelligence, ma'am," Simon acknowledged, with a solemn inclination of the head, and began to enjoy himself hugely. "I fear I do not aspire to such elevated circles."

"Well, I daresay it will fade rapidly enough in this bleak clime," Ann replied prosaically.

"Ay," agreed his lordship, "as will my lean look, too, after a month or so of Jules' fare."

At mention of the chef a smile hovered about her lips again, and Simon wondered if she were recalling her encounter with the snails, but she merely expressed her appreciation for the chef's help with the dinner.

They went on to converse easily on all manner of subjects, and Simon found to his surprise he was telling her how he had come to leave Branthorpe, although he did not mention Amelia's subsequent misfortunes. All too soon he found he had escorted her to the boundary wall of Shipton Grange. He jumped down, hitched Sinner's bridle to the ring by the great studded foor, and helped Miss Dorville dismount. She took the ribbons from him and led her chestnut horse back into her garden whilst his lordship held open the door.

"Thank you. I have really had a most enjoyable ride, my lord," Ann said, and favoured her companion with a dazzling smile which transported him straight back to the dining-room of the Swan.

"It was my pleasure, ma'am," he said, with a slight bow, and a lift to his crepe-swathed beaver hat.

As he rode back, he reflected that the sooner Miss Dorville was safely installed at Wragston Hall the better it would be for his peace of mind—and heart.

*   *   *

By the following morning it was obvious that Mr. Trant's fever attack was to be of short duration; he was much weakened by it, but when Simon looked in on the sick-room before breakfast he found he had passed a peaceful night and still seemed lethargic. His lordship did not disturb him, therefore, but was vastly relieved that his diagnosis appeared to have been correct.

It was a fine morning, and, on an impulse, Simon decided to take a ride before breakfast. The pleasant memory of the previous day's ride was not far from his mind and he found himself guiding Sinner along the same path again. He was somewhat taken aback, though, when he discovered Miss Dorville riding along the route too. Exchanging initially embarrassed greetings, they soon explained it to their own satisfaction as an extraordinary coincidence and went on to have another thoroughly enjoyable ride together.

But, by the time Simon returned to Branthorpe and was going into breakfast, he was more than a little perturbed and not inclined to regard it as entirely a chance meeting; he told himself sternly he would have to be more careful in his future dealings with his brother's fiancée.

John had not returned home yet and Simon found Amelia on her own in the breakfast parlour, seated with her back towards the door. She half-turned her head in response to her brother's greeting, and he went to the sidetable to help himself from the heated dishes. "Philip is much better this morning, Melly. It seems I was right."

"Oh good, I'm very pleased." Her response sounded sincere, but was given in such a subdued voice that her brother looked searchingly at her when he took his place at the table.

"Hey, what's amiss?" he asked gently, seeing her shadowed eyes, and face quite drained of colour. "Are you sickening for something, too?"

Amelia pressed her lips together and shook her head. "No, I didn't sleep too well, that's all," she replied quietly.

"Oh, come on Melly, there's more to it than that, I'll warrant! I've told you I will do my utmost to help over the child, so don't despair."

She took a sip of chocolate and seemed to have difficulty swallowing it. "Mama told me she had had a letter from Aunt Lennox."

"Oh damn. There was no call for her to do that," Simon exclaimed, annoyed.

"I guessed it had come when I saw the boy yesterday, and you could not expect her to lie when I asked about it," Amelia told him wearily.

"Did mama also tell you she had spoken to me of it?"

"Yes."

"Well then, I would have thought you might be pleased. She had promised not to act for the moment," Simon pointed out.

"She is not going to act at all, because *I* am. I decided last night," she said flatly.

Simon felt a decided misgiving at these words. "Oh, and what was that?" he asked, and went on calmly pouring some more coffee for himself.

"I suddenly realised that with the increased independence you have settled upon me now, I don't have to do what anyone tells me," Amelia said, with an unconcious jut of the chin. "I have enough to support the two of us—"

"But Melly," protested Simon, appalled that his small benefaction should have fostered such a notion, "where would you possibly live?" He forebore to mention that he *could* reduce the allowance again to the £500 left her by her father, as they were both aware he would do no such thing.

"Anywhere but here," she retorted defiantly. "I shall ask Betsy to come with me—she is my abigail after all—and I thought it would be nice if we could have one of the cottages at Wragston, but I see that it might pose problems for John."

"Problems!" exclaimed her brother, completely overcome.

"Well, I thought you would be pleased. After all, you want me to keep my baby, don't you? And this way I can, thanks to your generosity."

Simon groaned and drew his hand across his eyes.

"Melly, for God's sake be reasonable," he pleaded. "It is quite out of the question that you should set up house on your own. And as for Wragston—well! Can you imagine your wretched brother having you as his tenant?"

"If I bring no objection I see no reason why he should, but I own it might be a severe embarrassment for him," she conceded reluctantly. "In that case I may choose somewhere like Harrowgate where I am not known. Oh, don't worry, I shall use the name Morley."

"Well, of course I worry, Melly! I've never heard such gammon," Simon said, but not unkindly. His sister's schemes were obviously inspired by desperation; it was clear she had *not* resigned herself to losing the child at all, and the receipt of the letter had finally made her realise the fact. "Look, if you carry out this threat, you will forfeit your position and all chance of a reasonable marriage."

"The first I have already lost, and I am not really interested in the second. I have no wish to be rescued by some decrepit but indulgent nobleman discovered for me by mama," she declared in rising tones.

Quickly—and easily—quelling a brief desire to laugh, Simon merely said: "I beg you, just give me a little more time, and I promise that, even if I can't contrive a happy solution, I would as lief try to persuade mama to come about then lose you again."

Amelia stared fixedly at her distorted image in the silver chocolate pot. "You must see I don't *want* to leave but—" Her lip quivered, and she got no further. Picking up her spoon, she removed the skin carefully from the now cold chocolate.

Her brother deemed it wise to be silent for a while, and applied himself to finishing his breakfast. His meal completed, he rose, and as he went past his sister, placed a hand on her shoulder. "I know you think I'm incapable of bringing anything off right, but please don't do anything too scatter-brained just yet, will you Melly?"

There was no reply, but the fair, curly head shook slowly from side to side.

"But the by," said her brother in a different tone of voice, "does this niece of mine rejoice in a name? I cannot refer to her as 'she' for ever."

There was a long pause. "She didn't have—and you're not to tell anyone—but I've decided to call h-her P-Philippa," Amelia informed him, in stifled tones.

His lordship was looking very thoughtful indeed when he came out of the breakfast parlour, and Stagg intercepted him.

"I believe Mr. Featherstone was looking for you, m'lord," the butler said.

"Mm? Oh, thank you Stagg. He's in the office, is he? Well, don't worry, I will go to him," his lordship stated.

As Simon strode the long corridor to the steward's office, he reflected how little time he had had to himself since returning home. However, he was delighted to be back and would not have wished for a better way to spend his days than managing Branthorpe Park, but he did wonder how his sister occupied herself. He knew now, of course, why she had not had much social life when she returned, but could not help thinking it had been a mistake on his mother's part not to have encouraged her to go out more before his father had died. It was scarcely to be wondered at if she had become over-wrought after months of incarceration in this great house, with nothing save her intolerable situation to brood about. He suspected, also, that although little had been said, his sister's state of health had probably been very depressed for a considerable time after the birth. He resolved, there and then, to take steps towards helping her—that very day if it proved possible.

Luncheon was a quiet meal with just three of the family. The Dowager, after enquiring about Mr. Trant's progress, became immersed in a commonplace discussion concerning various Branthorpe tenants, of whose welfare Simon had enquired and whom he had, as yet, been unable to visit. Amelia seemed calmer again, but still lacked appetite and showed no interest in the conversation.

Upon quitting the dining-room, his lordship made directly for his friend's bedchamber, where he was pleased to see Philip propped up against the pillows, an empty tray beside him.

"Well, you old fraud, I see you are going along prosperously!" Simon said, beaming, as he removed the tray and placed it on the chest of drawers.

Philip smiled, albeit a little wanly. "Yes, I feel recruited after my interminable sleep. I think your man sought to render me senseless with the laudanum! But seriously, he had been a prodigious comfort—and so have you," Philip said, turning grateful eyes to his friend.

"Fudge!" retorted his lordship. "You must not exhaust yourself with these fulsome thanks. Here, let me set your pillows to right," he offered, and, all the while he was pummelling the feathers, he was endeavouring to calculate whether Philip had really recovered enough to be told about Amelia. "Let me feel that pulse," he requested, still unsure. "Mm, not bad, not bad at all," Simon commented presently, and he decided to take the risk considering what lay at stake.

"Phil, while you have been sequestered from the world up here, I have contrived to get to the root of that business of Amelia's locket." Simon was resting against the massive bedpost at the foot of the bed and, watching his friend carefully, he continued: "We were utterly out in our reckoning."

"Oh," said Philip, with a quick, apprehensive look, "how so?"

"There is no lover in the case, only a baby—Amelia's."

"Good Lord," Philip breathed, and there was no question that Simon now held his friend's attention; his fingers, which had been idly tracing the embroidered coronet on the sheet, were still.

Simon went on to tell him briefly what had happened since Amelia's return to Branthorpe and, as he did so, he became increasingly aware of how curious it must sound to his straighforward friend. "I'm afraid we must appear a ramshackle family," he remarked, with a short laugh. "We seem to get into the most amazing hobbles."

But Philip was not laughing. "That poor child," he said, almost to himself, and for a moment Simon did not know to whom he referred. But then he went on: "And what is to become of the infant? Adopted you said?"

When Simon nodded his friend murmured, with great depth of feeling: "No, no, that should not be." He raised unquiet eyes to Simon, and said quickly, "I'm sorry, I have no right to say that."

Now that Simon had taken the matter thus far, his resolution began to fail and he did not know how to proceed for the best. He left his position at the foot of the bed rather precipitately, and started to pace the Turkey carpet. "Phil, as you know, my influence on my sister has been little short of disastrous. No! it cannot be denied," he said as his friend started to murmur a protest, "and the last thing I wanted to do when I returned home was to interfere in the smallest degree in her life. After all, she is of age now and it should scarcely be necessary. But—well—I am now faced with this awful dilemma, for if I flout my mother's authority I may not be rendering any great service to Amelia. She would have to rear the child here, and I foresee a prospect of unending family friction," Simon paused for a moment, unnecessarily stirred the fire and put on another log.

"Is there no prospect of her marrying?" asked Philip. "It seems inconceivable to me that she is not besieged with eager suitors."

"You are forgetting, Phil, that her position is not a very enviable one. Admittedly, she has a competence now, and I shall see she does not lack a dowry, but this cannot make up for an illegitimate child and an immediate past which would not serve as best recommendations to a prospective husband."

"Stuff!" cried Philip from his pillows, which surprised his friend both by its force and uncharacteristic dismissal of another's viewpoint. "None of that is to the purpose, if I may say so. She is beautiful, intelligent, gentle, young—"

"Hey! Hold hard!" Simon begged, as this catalogue of virtues rolled on apparently unending. "I'll not deny my own sister's qualities—even if you do rather overstate the case," he said, smiling slightly, "but young she is not, when it comes to marriage. It is not to be supposed that she would have married later than her eighteenth year but for that act of utter folly! In fact her betrothal was being arranged with Lord Andover's eldest son at the time," his lordship reminded Philip, who was heard to sign rather violently.

"Yes, of course. I own I was disregarding her noble birth. I do see it would be most unfitting were she to wed a commoner."

"Oh no, you mistake me, Phil!" protested Simon hastily. "Why, it is no longer out of the way for us to

marry outside our own set. Witness my brother John!
And I certainly would not contemplate a *mariage de
convenance*. No, I merely wanted to indicate that her
opportunities of meeting a suitable partner are much
diminished. The London season is very much a marriage mart, you know, and that is not to be thought of
now in her situation."

There was silence in the room for a moment, broken
only by the kiss and roar of the green wood in the
grate as it was consumed by the flames. Simon went to
where the drugs and nostrums stood on the table, and
he started to examine them in an apparently idle manner. "No," he continued, as if there had been no pause.
"I would give my blessing to any fellow who would
love and cherish Amelia and her child." He selected a
small bottle of ruby liquid, removed the glass stopper
and held it, and a small vial, against the pale light fil-
tering through the window. "I suppose it must be this
stuff—it's dulled your senses or something, eh, Phil?"
he said, and stopped squinting at the glass for a moment to glance at his friend. Those spaniel-like eyes
were fixed upon him in some bewilderment. Simon returned to his alchemy, putting down the bottle and adding water to the vial from the carafe. "Dammit, I can't
make you offer for my sister! But then, I don't blame
you really," he said sympathetically, "I expect you're
set in your bachelor ways. Don't want petticoat govern-
ment at your advanced age, eh? Did you say something?" He asked blithely, turning and carrying the
potion over to the bed.

"Simon, you can't seriously be suggesting I should
marry Lady Amelia," Philip managed to gasp out at
last.

"We-ell, I did just have the tiniest suspicion you
might not find it a disagreeable prospect, but do,
please, correct me if I'm wrong."

Philip looked quite aghast at this flippancy. "This is no matter for jest. Of course, I should deem it the greatest honour to marry your sister, anybody would—"

"Ah no, Phil," objected his lordship, waving the glass about rather perilously to make his point. "There you are wrong, as I have just been at pains to point out." He thrust the potion under his friend's nose. "Here, I think you stand in need of this," he said, kindly.

Philip gulped it down obediently, choked a little, then said: "But what of Amelia's reaction to this? I cannot believe she had consented to this arrangement."

Simon looked a little graver at this. "No, she had not consented, for the simple reason that no proposal has yet been placed before her. However, I flatter myself that I diagnosed your feelings accurately enough, did I not?"

His friend directed his gaze down uncomfortably at his folded hands on the sheet, and said nothing.

"I have reason to think that your suit would be successful, although I cannot guarantee it. I am sorry, Phil, that it had to be done this way. Believe me, I thought very carefully, in my unaccustomed role of matchmaker, which of you to approach first, but it is better this way, I think. I could not risk raising my sister's hopes only to have the whole notion set aside by you."

"As if I would—" protested Philip, who was looking decidedly hectic now.

"No, maybe not, but do consider, there is the child of whom you knew nothing." At this juncture, Simon realised with some guilt that his friend was becoming quite overwrought with the combined effects of weakness and emotion. "I will leave you now, Phil, to rest and think about things. We'll talk about it again when you've slept on it."

And sleep he would, thought Simon, as he closed the door silently behind him, after twenty drops of laudanum.

SIXTEEN

IF THE Earl of Branthorpe considered he had experienced more than his fair share of emotional interviews for one day, few would gainsay him. Nevertheless, even as he sought refuge in the book-room after seeing Mr. Trant, a carriage was bowling up the drive conveying yet another disturbance into his ken, for Branthorpe was not the only house in the neighbourhood to have seen trouble that day.

Earlier, Ann Dorville had been with her mother in the chilly guest room recently vacated by Miss Merivale.

"It wasn't until I was supervising Maria as she set this room to rights yesterday, that I realised how shabby it has become," pronounced Mrs. Dorville, shaking a curtain like an enraged terrier. "This has faded monstrously and is now quite the wrong shade for the walls, don't you agree, my love?"

Ann was staring past the offending curtains and into the garden beyond. "Mm? Oh yes, quite wrong," she said unhelpfully.

Because of Ann's forthcoming marriage and subsequent departure from Shipton Grange, her mother was seeking her advice on various domestic matters before she left, although that event was still two months away at least.

Mrs. Dorville was undeterred by the half-hearted response, wanting only an audience at this stage for her own ideas. "I think I shall have some pattern books sent up. Pricket shall ride into York with my instructions and bring some back at once."

This was a procedure which normally would have wrung a protest from her daughter's lips on the squandering of servants' time, particularly as the small household was still disorganised after the party. This morning, though, Ann's mind was elsewhere. It was not, as might be expected, on her future husband who had driven off enthusiastically with a comparatively strange woman the day before, but on his brother. She had been unable to banish the memory of her encounter with his lordship the previous afternoon. She could not remember when she had enjoyed a ride more, and yet neither could she recall that anything outstandingly brilliant or entertaining had been said. She simply had felt utterly at ease with him in a way never experienced with John—or any other man. But then, remembering their more recent meeting this morning, she could not help feeling a little guilty.

Had her mother been aware of the direction of her daughter's thoughts she would have been jubilant and employed every means to encourage her, even taking John's "gallivanting" with a female—which she had already been heard to condemn roundly—as a reason for cancelling the betrothal. But by this time Mrs. Dorville had started vilifying the carpet. "I would have supposed this might resist the sun, but then blue is always a difficult colour," she said, eyeing the floor critically.

Mr. Dorville's raised voice was heard suddenly from the lower regions of the house.

"Now, what can he want?" exclaimed his wife crossly. "I do wish he would use the servants to convey messages instead of calling us in as if we were cattle."

Ann, knowing full well that her father normally spent his mornings quietly in his study and did not willingly seek out his spouse, was disturbed. "Something may be wrong, mama. We ought to go down."

"Oh, very well, but it's very tiresome of him."

As Ann looked down over the banister to the black and white marble of the hall, Mr. Dorville was standing there polishing his glasses in a frantic manner. He raised his head, and his daughter noticed at once his ruddy complexion had taken on a livid hue. "Papa, what's the matter?" she asked, gathering up her skirts and hastening towards him.

She was met with an unfocussed stare not wholly accounted for by the absence of spectacles. "Oh—er you'd both better come in here," he mumbled, indicating his small study. This unprecedented invitation was not reassuring.

Mrs. Dorville, who had been following her daughter at a more leisurely pace, now arrived on the scene. "Now, my dear sir, what is all this about?" she demanded imperiously.

"I think papa is not well," Ann told her in a hasty aside.

But Mr. Dorville overheard. "No, no," he retorted in agitated tones. "I'm perfectly all right if only I can find this damned letter. Oh, do you sit down, both of you," he said in exasperation, although the study only provided one hard chair besides his own leather one.

"Really, Mr. Dorville, what are you about? I cannot be expected to waste time like this," said his wife, ignoring his request.

As her mother was clearly not going to accept the offer of a chair, Ann decided she ought to, and at the same time said to her father tentatively, "Is the letter perhaps in your tail-coat pocket, papa?"

"Ah! That's it," he cried sharply, his usual good humour still notably lacking. He spread the missive on the desk before him and stood looking down in a gloomy manner. "Well, you'll have to know sometime, I suppose," he sighed. "And so it is better if I tell you the worst now."

By this time even his wife had realised that all was not well, and had stopped pacing the meagre floor space, to her daughter's great relief.

Ann, who had recognised the letter heading as that of her father's London bank, guessed what might be coming, and stood up very slowly again, her attention on her mother.

"Not to put too fine a point on it, we're most likely ruined," Mr. Dorville said bluntly. "The bank in which I had most of your money lodged, my dear, has failed." He cast a despairing glance at his daughter, but the reaction came from his wife, who made a curious wailing noise and subsided into the chair, helped by the swift assistance of Ann.

The rest of that painful scene was still vivid in Ann's mind as, with her father, they now approached Branthorpe Park in their carriage. Her mother, usually inordinately proud of her robust health, and contemptuous of the vapours in others, had had to be put to bed by Ann and Maria, and soothed by some hitherto much desposed lavender drops, fetched from the servants' quarters: but it was her father who was causing Ann

the most concern. She had do her best to convince him
that she did not regard it herself as the end of the
world. As far as she could ascertain from her shattered
parent, the family would still have enough to live modestly where they were, but any thought of proceeding
with the marriage plans was presumably out of the
question, as it was her own, recently inherited fortune
which had melted away. She realised now what had
been worrying her father before the dance, and also
why he had bought the diamonds. She had suspected,
only, that it was to give her something that John would
be unable to dispose of easily.

Mr. Dorville had wished to visit Branthorpe on his
own, but had not had enough spirit to object when
Ann insisted on accompanying him; she had not considered it wise to let him travel alone in his oppressed
and shocked state of mind, as she feared a reaction.

It was not until they were within a hundred yards of
their destination that Ann realised what a dreadful or-
deal the visit might prove to be for her, as well as for
her father. His intention was to see John, who, they assumed, would be home again by now; and Ann had
hoped to spend the time with Lady Amelia. But perhaps an encounter with John would be unavoidable,
she reflected, and because she did not know how he
might react she was very apprehensive. If he loved her
as he had professed, he was surely going to be more
wretched about the failure of their marriage plans than
she was? Her thoughts were still in a state of tumult
when the carriage door was opened. Not a word had
passed between father and daughter throughout the
short journey, but she gave him a quick, somewhat
tremulous smile as she prepared to step down.

*   *   *

His lordship had difficulty in suppressing a groan when Staff informed him that Mr. Thomas Dorville was desirous of seeing him.

"His business lies with Mr. John, I understand, m'lord, but when I informed Mr. Dorville he was from home, I noticed the said gentleman seemed to be labouring under great perturbation of spirits, and I deemed it advisable to seek you out at once, m'lord."

God! Stagg was a prosy old fool at times, thought Simon impatiently; and it did not sound remotely like Mr. Dorville's normal behaviour either.

"I have shown them into the Blue Saloon, m'lord," added the butler.

"Them!" ejaculated Simon, thinking that the only thing the day had lacked so far was an encounter with Mrs. Dorville.

"Miss Dorville is accompanying her father, m'lord."

Simon relaxed a little. "Well, show Mr. Dorville in here, Stagg, and you had best ask Lady Amelia to entertain the daughter." The Dowager would be resting, as always, after luncheon and would not wish to be disturbed.

"That won't be possible as m'lady left in the carriage shortly after luncheon," Stagg informed him with a certain relish, or so it seemed to his hard-pressed master.

"Where was she bound for, do you know?" enquired Simon, trying to surpress the anxiety he felt over this unexpected news, as various alarming possibilities flitted through his mind; he remembered Amelia's reserved behaviour at luncheon.

"That I cannot say, m'lord."

"Oh, well," sighed his lordship wearily, "see to it that Miss Dorville has everything she needs in the Blue Saloon, Stagg, and show Mr. Dorville in here," he repeated. The butler vouchsafed no response to this implied aspersion on his initiative, and retreated.

Ann refused the offer of refreshment made by the
butler, but when her father had been absent for almost
half an hour, her mouth was so dry she regretted her
decision. They had clearly chosen a most inconvenient
time to call, and she remembered, too, that the Frensham guest, Mr. Trant, lay sick. She wished now she
had exercised more restraint on her father and persuaded him to let their York attorney deal with the
matter in a more formal manner. As she was consoling
herself that at least she would not have to face John
today, she found herself summoned by the butler into
the presence of Lord Branthorpe and her father.

Entering the book-room with some degree of despondency and not a little embarrassment, Ann was
struck at once by the almost cheerful aspect of his
lordship as he greeted her, and the vastly improved appearance of her father, whose complexion had regained
its normal ruddiness. Mr. Dorville was sitting by the
fire, not entirely at his ease, but with a brandy at his
elbow. Ann was escorted by his lordship to a chair opposite her father, and provided with a glass of
Madeira.

"Well, this is sad news, indeed, Miss Dorville," began Simon, "but I have been trying, and I hope with
some success, to persuade your father that things may
not be as bad as they first appear. Bank failures have
become all too familiar of late, as my attorney informed me only recently, but in a great many cases as
much as fourteen shillings in the pound can finally be
paid out. I should be surprised if something of this order were not the case in this instance. It is not to be
supposed that this will happen overnight, of course—
these things take time. Nevertheless it would be a mistake, I feel, to take too despairing a view at this early
stage," he said encouragingly.

Ann was both gratified and surprised that Lord

Branthorpe should include her in this masculine discussion; she had expected only embarrassing platitudes. "That is good news indeed, is it not, papa?"

Mr. Dorville cleared his throat rather noisily. "Yes, I own that perhaps I was too hasty in my conclusions. I should not have flown here at once, clucking like a hen deprived of her brood, and worrying his lordship with it all."

Ann feared that this wild image might prove too much for Lord Branthorpe, who certainly did not seem too castdown by their tidings, but he controlled his features admirably.

"Oh no, not at all, sir, you did quite the best thing. I'm sure my brother will be most grateful for your direct dealing in the matter," Simon assured his guest.

Mr. Dorville looked thoughtful, leaning forward slightly in the chair, his huge hands spread on his knees. "Ay well, Mr. Frensham has always been very open with me, my lord, and it seemed only right he should know at once, without any shilly-shally. It puts quite a different complexion on the Settlement, there's no denying that; and my girl will have to—"

Ann was relieved when their host cut across this line of speculation.

"As to that, sir, it is for my brother to decide," Simon said.

"Quite right! Forgive me, my lord, my wits have gone a'begging since this morning, I fear," apologised a flustered Mr. Dorville.

"It must have been a severe shock indeed, sir, and I do sympathise," said his lordship kindly.

"Maybe," agreed Mr. Dorville, "but there is no call for us to take up any more of your time. You have been a great help, my lord, and I do appreciate our little talk." He drew himself to his feet, and Ann, after hastily swallowing her wine, also rose.

"My brother is expected back at any moment, and he will doubtless be in touch with you, sir," said Simon, as he tugged the bell-rope for Stagg to show the visitors out.

Ann would like to have thanked Lord Branthorpe particularly for restoring her father's spirits so skilfully, but she had only the opportunity to offer a formal "thank you" as they left.

In less than five minutes after his guests's departure, Simon had sought out the Dowager in her room. Without any preamble, he asked: "Mama where has Amelia gone?"

She looked up from her needlework. "I gave her permission to take the carriage into York for the afternoon. Betsy is with her."

"Are you certain that is where she was intending to go?" asked her son suspiciously.

"Oh really, Simon," chided the Dowager, resuming her sewing. "The poor child scarcely ever leaves the house, and I was delighted to see her take an interest in a little shopping for a change." She paused for a moment. "I thought I heard a carriage earlier. Who was it?"

Simon told her of the Dorville news.

"Well! You knew that, and all you can talk about is your sister's whereabouts." Her needle was arrested once more. "I'll warrant that marks an end to Master John's passion," she said trenchantly.

"But it may not make a vast difference to the ultimate outcome, as I tried to reassure Mr. Dorville," objected Simon.

"Perhaps not, but I am persuaded your brother will consider he has languished for his heiress long enough. He lacks patience, you know," his parent commented dispassionately.

Simon, who had very mixed feelings on this latest

development in John's affairs, offered no further opinion, but said presently: "Mama, I think you should know the scheme I have afoot for Amelia, because it may help to have your approbation."

"Oh, I am flattered. I had supposed my wishes to be of little import," the Dowager said with a tolerant smile.

"I'm sorry if I have seemed high-handed, mama," Simon apologised, "but I think this may have been all for the best, if Amelia agrees, of course. You see, Mr. Trant wishes to marry her—indeed I have rarely seen a fellow so besotted," chuckled his lordship.

"Nor have I," retorted the Dowager drily. "But I was afraid his sudden illness might throw an interminable delay over the affair."

Her son gave her a startled look. "You knew?" he exlaimed.

"Well, naturally, you great gudgeon! Anyone who had eyes to see would know! Why else do you think I appealed to you for help finally? You were the obvious person to bring Mr. Trant to the point."

Simon took a moment to digest this information, then recovering, asked: "You think Amelia will consent?"

The Dowager nodded, her eyes closing briefly. "I think so. I have watched her closely, too, and I would not go so far as to say she is in love with him. I think she had been hurt too recently to allow her heart to rule her head at the moment, but, yes, I do think she will agree. And personally I could not wish for a better outcome."

"Of course," said Simon ruefully, "I was so convinced of her interest in young Lambert that, beyond realising that she seemed to like Philip well enough, I attached no importance to her reaction until recently."

"Yes, it has been hard on you, I know," sympathised his mother. "But whilst you have been closeted with Featherstone and Cuffe, I have seen Amelia and your friend dealing famously together. I think it will all come right yet."

"It may," agreed her son quietly, "if Amelia returns."

But even this ominous prognostication did not appear to disturb the Dowager. "If? How should she not return?" she asked in a mild manner.

"She was talking wildly this morning of taking the child and setting up a separate establishment, and Lord knows what else," Simon told her.

"Well, I warrant she'll not get far with the scheme this afternoon," the Dowager chuckled. "I took the liberty of giving Sam Coachman particular orders to drive direct to York and home again. He dotes on Amelia like a father you know, alway has. Anyway," continued his mother complacently, "where would she go? You must not suppose that just such a possibility had not occurred to me, now that she is in possession of an independence. But she would need the connivance of someone and, on this occasion, I am persuaded you would not be a willing accomplice," she averred, with a slow smile.

His lordship gave strong corroboration to this supposition. "Well, of course not! I did all in my power to put the scatter-brained scheme out of her head." He laughed suddenly. "Mama, I think you need no help from me at all! I could have stayed in India."

"No, I think you do yourself an injustice there," his mother said reflectively. "You see, Amelia would never have made the acquaintance of Mr. Trant had you not returned home," the Dowager explained, her eyes kindling; then she took up her embroidery again.

SEVENTEEN

THE DOWAGER Countess's confidence in her ability to control her daughter's activities was not entirely well-founded. Amelia had spent her afternoon buying clothing and other necessities for her baby, which, in normal circumstances, would have been made by herself and the Branthorpe servants long before the birth. Upon her arrival home, the results of her expenditure involved the footman in three laden journeys to her room, but these went unobserved by her family and, in any event, she had taken care to include some purchases for herself.

Thus, when Simon saw her first at dinner wearing a new indigo velvet gown, he felt somewhat reassured that her expedition had been innocent. The rich dark blue set off her golden hair and fair colouring, and she looked more attractive than he ever remembered, but sadly she still had a rather tense and unhappy air. He found himself hoping that his mother would broach the subject of Philip's offer with her that evening; for it had been settled that the suggestion should come from her and not Simon.

When the ladies left Simon to himself after dinner he

had the decanter carried up to Philip's room. His friend was much refreshed after his deep sleep and now apparently very inspirited by the prospect before him. So much so, that his lordship felt constrained to remind him that Amelia had not yet given her consent. However, Simon was unable to dispel Philip's sanguine mood entirely, for he was pleased simply to be feeling better, and also to know that Lady Amelia was not intending to contract another unsuitable marriage; he was convinced that if she were just allowed to keep the child she could not fail to be happier.

Simon could not share his optimism and when, on leaving Philip's room, he collided with his sister in the gallery outside, his spirits sank further. She was hurrying along, half-blinded with tears. Although she ignored him completely, Simon followed her to her room where she collapsed into a chair and sobbed. Her brother waited, embarrassed, and had ample time to notice, with no great degree of surprise, the small mountain of infant clothing strewn about the bed.

When she could speak finally, she said in a low, bitter voice: "It's all your doing, but I won't have Mr. Trant duped in this way. You and mama have dragooned him into it! Oh, I can see how opportune it all seemed, but I'm surprised at *you,* Simon, he's your friend."

All this was so far from the truth that all Simon could do was protest. "But it's not in the least like that, Melly—"

She ignored him. "He can't possibly want to marry me, and take responsibility for a child he's never seen! Why, he has not been here for much more than a sennight, and now he's ill and you're taking the opportunity to go behind his back with your wicked stratagems!"

"Melly, stop it, you're being hysterical!" commanded

her brother, sharply, although in fact he was relieved that she had not given the slightest indication so far that *she* would not marry Philip; he thought his mother had either sadly mismanaged the affair, or, more likely, Amelia had not given her time to explain anything. It seemed they had made a grave error of judgement in not letting Mr. Trant speak for himself; however, that was easily remedied. "I can assure you that Philip comprehends the situation perfectly. He is much better today, and was in high gig when I left him just now." For the first time, Amelia raised her head and looked, with reddened eyes, at her brother. "I have no intention of usurping his right to tell you why he is so bent on making you his wife," Simon said, smiling. "Besides, if you don't stop acting like a watering-pot even he might change his mind—although I doubt anything could, frankly. He's wonderfully moonstruck, poor fellow!" he added in wry accents. "But, let him speak for himself, won't you Melly? I swear he's not at the point of my sword—far from it!"

Whilst her brother had been speaking, Amelia had made ineffectual attempts to dry her eyes. "But I can't go in like this!" she objected feebly, still snuffling.

Simon soon brushed this protest aside. "You look wonderful. Come, splash some cold water, or whatever, on your face," he bade her unromantically. "I will go and tell him you are coming."

"Oh, but—" cried Amelia to her brother's retreating back.

However, Simon found her tolerably composed when he came back, and, casting all propriety to the winds, he thrust her into Philip's bedchamber, shut the door, and went downstairs. After summoning Joliffe and telling him Mr. Trant did not wish to be disturbed on any account, he joined his mother and explained what he had done. In view of her own lack of success, the

Dowager offered no objection to this unconventional proceeding, merely remarking, somewhat laconically, that it was up to Mr. Trant now; whereupon she returned to her novel.

Her son sank back into a chair, then idly picked up the newly-arrived copy of the *Gentleman's Magazine*. It failed lamentably in engaging his attention for, some time later, he had not progressed beyond the list of contents. Having spirited John out of the way, he now was wishing him back again. Although not relishing the task of reporting the Dorville bank failure to him, he did want to know if John intended to stand by his earlier avowals of affection. Miss Dorville would be bound to offer to cry off in the circumstances, he hazarded, and it would be left to his brother to make the final decision. Simon had been uncomfortably aware of a definite feeling of satisfaction upon hearing that Miss Dorville was bereft of the bulk of her fortune, but he realised now that it was unlikely to mean that he could step straight into his brother's shoes and claim the lady for his own. It was not to be supposed that John would tolerate having both fortune and bride snatched from him by the unlooked-for return of his elder brother. Difficult though it may be, he must not seen to influence John although he was convinced the match was unsuitable. What would John do? Simon wondered. It was the greatest pity that his brother had spent the last few years masquerading as the heir, instead of following a career of his own. However, the blame for that lies, once again, at my own door, thought Simon. There seemed to be no end to the ramifications of his absence from home, brief though it now appeared to him in retrospect.

Presently the drawing-room door opened quietly, and Amelia came in. Going straight to her mother, she put her arms round the Dowager's neck and kissed her on the cheek. "Thank you, mama," she said huskily, and with an uncertain smile hovering on her lips.

"I take it then that you have accepted Mr. Trant after all," the Dowager observed rather gruffly. "But don't thank me, my dear, he's the one responsible, you know." She nodded her widow's cap in the direction of Simon.

"Ma'am," retorted her son, a trifle sternly. "I have just spent some time convincing this gooscap that *neither* of us had any hand in this, and now you are quite destroying my efforts." Nevertheless, he accepted a kiss from his sister with a good grace, murmuring complacently, "I told you so, didn't I, Melly?"

"I still can't believe it," Amelia said, sitting on the edge of the sofa in a dazed manner.

"If *you* cannot, then I hesitate to think how Philip feels," Simon laughed. "Come, let me get you both a drink—this is something to celebrate indeed!"

Whilst her brother was busy with the decanters, Amelia spoke to her mother. "Mr. Trant would like to see baby, mama. C-can I fetch her home now?" she asked shyly.

"Yes, I suppose so," answered her mother, with only slight hesitation. "But you must make some preparations first, naturally. You'll need clothes and all manner of knick-kancks—I've almost forgotten, I'm afraid, what is needed," the Dowager said vaguely. "The old cradle is doubtless somewhere about. Mrs. Pringle will know where, I daresay," she went on, gradually warming to the subject. "Thank you," she acknowledged, as Simon placed a glass on the table at her side.

Amelia gave her brother a quelling look as he handed her a glass of wine.

"I expect you will find Amelia has the preparations made in no time at all, mama," forecast Simon, undeterred. "But, tell me, what tale are you going to concoct this time to explain the sudden reappearance of a baby in our midst?"

"I shall not concoct any tale," said the Dowager loftily, evidently deciding to put a bold face on things. "It is not of the least consequence what the servants—or anyone else—think now."

"If you want a plausible explanation for almost anything you should ask Simon," interjected Amelia, with a surprisingly mischievous look in her eye. "He's as good as Mrs. Radcliffe."

"Well, let me see," offered her brother promptly, endeavouring to oblige, although he guessed there was little the servants didn't know already. "Yes, you could always say she is Philip's daughter—as, of course, she will be." Then, because he was afraid Amelia might see this as a reminder of Philip's dead child, he said hastily: "Does he know her name yet, Melly?"

His sister shook her head repressively, but the Dowager put down her glass and said in surprised tones: "But she has no name, surely?"

"I know you told me I mustn't give her one, mama, but I have only this minute decided upon it—she's to be Philippa," Amelia explained, telling only a small white lie.

Simon smiled at her over the top of his glass.

"I see," murmured the Dowager, a trifle taken aback now by the pace of events; and before she had time to object to this name on the grounds that Mr. Trant might wish to name a future son Philip, her own younger son suddenly erupted into the room.

It seemed to Simon that John's arrival always had a turbulent effect on any gathering, and this occasion was no exception.

"Ah, too late for dinner, I see! No matter, I expect you'll be wanting tea sent in soon," announced the newcomer, his cheeks glowing, and seeming to bring a gust of cold air with him as he strode over to the bell-pull. "Hello, are we celebrating something?" he asked, observing that both his mother and sister had glasses—an unusual occurrence.

"Yes, John we are," the Dowager informed him happily. "Your sister's betrothal."

John looked startled. "What? By Jupiter! Who is it? Trant?"

It was Amelia's turn to look astonished. "Oh, not you too, John! It seems I was the only one not expecting this," she said with a sigh.

"Well, dash it, who else could it be? Still he's a devilish fast mover—"

"John," said Simon, with a minatory look, "I suggest we repair to the book-room. You can have your feast sent in to you there. I'm sure the ladies will be glad of a *tête-à-tête*."

"Oh yes, all right," replied his brother easily. "I say I do think it's capital news, truly," he told Amelia with a cheerful grin before he left.

"Thank you, John," Amelia replied, smiling at him for a moment, then watching solemnly as Simon followed to tell him the news concerning his fiancée.

Simon thought it would be a tactical error to introduce the subject before his ravenous brother had eaten, and, in any event, John was too busy telling him about his stay at Little Sutton.

"It was damned lucky really—Gerard Winthorpe was home on leave from his regiment. He's old Winthorpe's second son, you know, a Brigade Major with the Cavalry which is serving in the Peninsular at present. Only allowed home because of family trouble—his eldest brother seemed about to turn up his toes, but naturally by the time Gerard arrived, he was as hearty as a buck again," said John ingenuously.

At this point, Simon was tempted to make some

comment on the universal lack of consideration shown
by elder brothers for their juniors, but thought better
of it; and anyway John's narrative continued unabated.

"—Wellington's hard pressed out there at the moment. Short of good officers, apparently. Ah! food at
last!" he cried eagerly as Stagg came in with a laden
tray.

Simon, although he had never heard of Gerard Winthorpe until that minute, was eternally grateful to him,
as he was the means of showing him what should be
done about his brother.

Whilst John, seated at the desk which was serving as
a temporary dining-table, helped himself liberally to
the viands supplied by the butler, Simon took the opportunity to ask about Miss Merivale.

"Oh yes, she's quite fit now. Dashed boring female
though," he said rolling his eyes expressively ceilingwards. "Still, it was worth suffering a bit of such
cordial introduction to the Winthorpes. Oh sorry, I
seem to remember she said something about knowing
you for ever," he added, chewing unconcernedly.

"Yes, she would," responded his brother in sardonic
tones, "but don't fret. I am entirely of your opinion,"
Simon was vastly relieved that Clarissa Merivale appeared to have quit the scene now, leaving both his
brother and himself unscathed.

John soon returned with gusto to Major Winthorpe
and his part in Wellington's victory earlier in the year
at Salamanca.

Simon watched his brother's eyes shine, as he related
these exploits, in a way in which they had never
kindled when he spoken, albeit in enthusiastic terms, of
his future with Ann.

Presently, when John brought his tankard of ale and
stood by the hearth, his lordship decided it was time
for him to speak. "I shouldn't have let you run on like

this, John, I suppose, but you've obviously had a famous time of it, and I hesitate to spoil it."

John caught the foreboding tone, and eyed his brother suspiciously over the tankard. "Hey, you make it sound as though I'm to make ready for my cere-cloth at any moment?" he protested. "I thought there was something smoky afoot when you suggested this parley. You're not going to read me a lecture, are you?"

"No, nothing of that sort, but I do have some bad news, I'm afraid."

"Oh, not another lopping of my paltry income," groaned John.

"Not yours, John, but Miss Dorville's," said his brother succinctly.

"You're hoaxing me," responded John unsteadily, and placed the tankard on the mantel shelf. As Simon told him of Dorville's visit, John glowered. "I don't believe it—it's a sham to bamboozle me out of the full Settlement because my contribution has been curtailed!"

"You would not have thought so had you seen that poor old boy today, John—he was cut to pieces. Besides, you must know him better than that—there's not the smallest hint of knavery about him," protested Simon, taken aback by this wholly unwarranted attack on Mr. Dorville. "He will doubtless show you the letter which makes it plain enough."

"Oh, this is beyond anything," snapped John. "And he'll not show me any letter because as far as I am concerned the whole thing is off."

Simon raised his brows at this apparent evidence that his brother was a fortune-hunter. "But you will surely want to see him—and Miss Dorville—whatever the outcome? I am persuaded she will be quite prepared to cry off in the circumstances, but I understood you loved the girl," said Simon, unwillingly drawn into discussing the marriage, as he had vowed he would not be.

"Of all the infernal luck!" his brother fumed, ignoring Simon's exhortations. "But then the whole thing has been ill-fated from the start," he added morosely.

"Look, as I explained to Dorville, it may not make a deal of difference in the long term," averred his lordship, determined not to be guilty of influencing John to abandon Miss Dorville.

"No, I've had enough," John stated categorically. Then with an odd laugh, he added, "I'm damned if I wanted to settle down anyway."

As this sudden *volte-face* on the part of his brother would produce the precise outcome which Simon had been secretly wishing for, he took it with a greater degree of indulgence than would otherwise have been possible. "And what *did* you want to do?" he asked quietly, but as he looked at John's fierce expression and military-style sidewhiskers he could scarcely doubt the answer.

John shrugged. "Oh, what's that to the purpose?"

"On the contrary, I think it very much to the purpose, John. You must do something with your life. No! I'm not proposing to sermonise," he said placatingly. "But if I'd not gone away and left you expecting to step into my shoes, I suspect things would have fallen out quite differently. What say you to a pair of colours?" asked Simon abruptly, thus relinquishing his promise to himself not to sway his brother's decision, because now he felt quite convinced the marriage was a lost cause.

John looked down warily at him. "I'm damned if I know how you guessed, but anyway it costs a fortune," he said in depressed tones.

Simon laughed. "It needed no soothsayer, John, believe me! And I am persuaded it need not cost a fortune."

"But how can I go away? Even though you *have* come home now, something must be done with Wragston or I'll have no income worthy of the name."

Simon stared pensively at his brother. "I own I haven't given the scheme much consideration. Everything seems to be happening in the twinkling of a bedpost today. What with Amelia's betrothal and—" he broke off, then said with sudden enthusiasm: "How would it be John—and don't leap down my throat, I'm only thinking aloud—if you were to let Amelia and Philip have Wragston during your absence?"

"But does Trant know anything of estate management?" asked John slowly, but evidently much struck.

"As to that, I know his worth as an administrator, and I'll warrant the tenants would take to him. Melly, of course, they would know slightly anyway."

John's fair brows puckered. "It would still take almost all of a thousand pounds you know—to buy a commission in the Cavalry, I mean."

Simon grinned at him. "That's all right John, I hadn't thought you would accept a line regiment! But don't fret, I'll buy you a commission gladly, if that's what you want."

For once his brother didn't fly into a passion at the offer of help from him. "Well, I don't know, it's all a bit unexpected to tell the truth." He rubbed his forehead in a bewildered way. "It's dashed obliging of you—"

"Gammon!" said Simon, reflecting guiltily that it almost amounted to buying his brother out of the way of Miss Dorville. "You are quite certain about renouncing your marriage plans, are you?" he felt constrained to ask.

"Oh Lord, yes," responded his brother dismissively.

"I say Simon," he said with a sudden gleam in his eye. "I know this is a monstrous nerve, but you recollect you offered me a hunter as a wedding gift? Well, do you think I could have one still to take with me to the Peninsula? Wellington runs a pack of hounds there, you know."

"The devil he does!" ejaculated his lordship. "I'll tell you what," he said presently, in confidential tones. "you shall have Sinner—then Boney's as good as routed, I'll warrant!"

EIGHTEEN

"A NOTE has just arrived from Branthorpe, my love, directed to your father," said Mrs. Dorville, coming into the morning room at Shipton Grange, and looking more subdued than her daugher could ever recall seeing her.

It was scarcely four-and-twenty hours since the bank's letter had been received. The whole Dorville family had risen early that morning, and when her mother complained of a sleepless night, Ann had no grounds for doubting her word on this occasion.

Ann found the situation more of an embarrassment than a disaster. Despite Lord Branthorpe's kind assurances the previous day, she insisted that she must withdraw from the engagement at once, and a message had been despatched to their attorney to this effect. She considered it would be quite wrong to place John in the position of having to cry off, though mercifully, even now, there had been no official announcement.

"Are you still resolved to reject John, should he be prepared to continue with the betrothal?" asked her mother in mournful, but incredulous tones; all hopes of an even better match being quite abandoned by her now.

"Yes mama, quite resolved," replied Ann firmly. She could not explain that if this had happened before John's brother had returned she would most likely have felt differently.

Her mother fetched a theatrical sign, one of many that morning. "I can't help but blame your father for all this. He should have removed the money from the bank before this happened," she said critically.

"Papa did everything possible," Ann retorted, leaping to his defence. "He wanted to re-invest the money when it was made over to my name, but you know the banker is an old friend of his, and he begged papa not to do so. It would have aggravated the parlous state the bank was in at the time, and merely made matters worse."

"Not for us, it wouldn't," stated her mother flatly. "How could it be worse?"

"Oh, in many ways. Remember papa did put some of the money into the diamonds—"

"Five thousand pounds at the most! What is that but a drop in the ocean out of sixty thousand?"

"Yes, I know some of papa's money was lost as well as mine, but whatever is paid out ultimately by the bank he shall have it. I have no desire to deprive him of that. Together with the interest from his investments in the Funds, I am convinced you will be able to maintain a comfortable mode of life," Ann pointed out reasonably.

"But the shame!" cried her mother. "And what of you? With no dowry worth the name, how are we to find a husband for you?"

Ann was quite unmoved by this true but unflattering statement, as she reflected sadly that no dowry, however fabulous, was likely to enable her to marry the Earl. She was saved from having to answer this home question by the appearance of her father, who seemed in some indefinable way to have diminished in physical stature since the previous morning.

He addressed his daughter in a diffident manner. "Well, that seems to be it, I'm afraid, kitten. I've just heard from Mr. Frensham and the Settlement is to be nullified."

Ann felt a great sense of release on hearing this, but her mother said: "Spare us the legal niceties, Mr. Dorville! What you are saying is that your daughter has been cast aside for the sake of a few pounds!" she declared, promptly contradicting her earlier statements without so much as a blush.

"Mama! That is an outrageous exaggeration," protested Ann. "Does John say anything else, papa?" she asked, wondering how he had taken the news.

Mr. Dorville looked thoroughly discomfited. "No, he mentions only that he is going to be away for a time and his attorney will deal with everything."

"There! I'll warrant he's after that Merivale gel already! Her father is a nabob, I've heard. Well, that settles it! I'll not stay in this neighbourhood to be mocked, my dear sir."

The matter of renting Shipton Grange for a year or two had come up briefly the previous day, and had been deferred until John's decision was known. Ann was in agreement with her mother in wishing to move, but for quite another reason; she wanted to forget Lord Branthorpe as quickly as possible. Where they should go was of perfect indifference to her, and she ignored the ensuing argument between her parents on the merits of north versus south, and town versus country.

A decision was made, however, that the Grange should be found a tenant at the first opportunity. In order that this should be settled by Christmas, which was quite near now, Mr. Dorville and his daughter set out for York the following day to put matters in hand.

Mrs. Dorville stayed at home, saying bitterly she saw no point in going near any shops if there was no money to spend. Ann was pleased to accompany her father as it meant she could get out of the house for a while; since calling at Branthorpe Park two days before she had not gone out riding in case she should meet with Lady Amelia or, more particularly, Lord Branthorpe. She felt none of the sense of shame which afflicted her mother, but nevertheless thought a meeting would be attended by a degree of awkwardness which she had rather avoid.

It was a bleak day and the overhung sky gave every indication of snow to come; no one would be abroad who did not have compelling reasons for travelling, and Ann felt confident, therefore, that she would encounter no neighbours in York.

As soon as they arrived, they left their carriage in the stables of the Swan posting-house as usual and partook of a late luncheon there.

"It seems incredible, doesn't it, papa, that it is not yet two weeks since we first saw Lord Branthorpe here?" she remarked, looking wistfully at the table he and his friend had occupied, and which was not taken by two dull, professional-looking gentlemen in Brutus wigs.

"Ay, kitten, it does," sighed her father. "I own I'll be sorry to leave my good neighbours behind, but somehow since the old Earl died everything has changed, and mighty quickly too. Not that I would say a word against his heir; I think we would have dealt very well together," he said regretfully.

"Do we have to go, papa?" Ann asked, because although she did not mind for herself now, she was sorry her father was being uprooted from the home where he had intended spending the rest of his days.

"Oh, I shouldn't worry for myself, perhaps, but your mother would find it difficult to retrench if we stay, I know. And a change won't do us any harm, I daresay; at least until we know where we stand again," he declared bracingly. "I only hope I can get someone who will look after my succession houses properly, though," he added, suddenly cast down again.

Ann accompanied her father to the door of the house agent's office and then, as he was intending to visit his attorney and his man of business afterwards, she left him and proceeded to the Circulating Library. She staye there in the warmth until she thought her father would be near completing his business, then left to walk back slowly to the Swan.

Her heart suddenly missed a beat as she saw the unmistakable tall figure of Lord Branthorpe approaching on the same side of the narrow street. However, she felt sure he had not seen her as he was walking into the wind and was obliged to bend his head and hold his beaver hat secure. She darted into the nearest doorway and found to her chagrin it was the print shop. The entrance was shallow and afforded little protection, and she realised also that she was wearing the same grey velvet walking dress of their first meeting.

But in any event, his lordship stopped and looked in the window. "Miss Dorville! Well, this is a pleasure!"

His face which, Ann noticed, had seemed dejected, brightened considerably.

"Good afternoon, Lord Branthorpe," she replied, irrationally pleased now that he had spoken to her. They both glanced at the hunting scenes displayed before them, and smiled quickly at each other. Then, because she felt some reference ought to be made to his gift, she murmured, feeling rather foolish: "They are fine, are they not?"

"Indeed," answered his lordship readily, "I should have given you the whole set."

"Oh no—"

"May I escort you anywhere? I am merely passing the time until the London coach arrives," he explained.

"I was making my way to the Swan to await my father. But are you going away, too, my lord?" she was surprised into asking, whilst thinking that if he was leaving Branthorpe she would have no pressing need to.

He turned to retrace his footsteps with her. "Oh no, I am meeting a friend who I hope will be on the coach." Then in an altered voice he said: "I'm afraid it must seem very hard for you to understand John's precipitate action."

"Oh, not at all! My father had already taken steps to curtail the betrothal," she assured him in prosaic tones.

"No, I meant more particularly his decision to join Gerard Winthorpe in his cavalry regiment, but I expect he would discuss this with you yesterday before he left."

Ann was startled to hear this. "But I have not seen him? He has already left, you say? For a cavalry regiment? You must be hoaxing me!" she cried but, although she had reason to think her companion had a lively sense of humour, she did not suppose he would indulge it on this topic. Certainly, he did not look amused as his step checked momentarily.

"This is no hoaxing matter, Miss Dorville! Do you mean to tell me that that wretched boy did not call upon you after all?" his lordship said rashly. "Oh, this is beyond anything!" He resumed walking, his sensitive mouth set grimly.

Ann hazarded from this outburst that John may have disobeyed his brother's injunctions in the matter, and it followed, probably, that his lordship was privy to his brother's sentiments. She decided to be frank as she had little to lose now. "I expect he would have found the encounter embarrassing in the extreme. I certainly should! So do not blame him for that. But I hope you can set my mind at ease on one point, though; it is not a broken-heart which has prompted this unlooked-for action, I hope?" she asked, tolerably certain that it was not so, but there was no denying he had been very convincing in his role of lover recently.

His lordship's expression throughout this brief speech had changed from one of annoyance to that of acute discomfort, Ann observed. "Forgive me, Lord Branthorpe, I see I have placed you in an invidious position with my clumsy enquiries," she put in quickly.

"No, Miss Dorville, I fear it is my brother who has placed me in an invidious position, as you put it," said his lordship ruefully. "He seems to have behaved very badly, and I must in all honesty say that he appeared regrettably heart-whole when last I spoke with him." He looked anxiously at his companion for her reaction to this unflattering news.

"Oh well, that's a blessing anyway," she cried cheerfully.

This seemed to afford his lordship some measure of relief. "You appear to be facing your misfortune with admirable spirit, if I may say so, Miss Dorville," he commented tentatively.

"Oh, pray do not mistake me!" Ann protested, realising that her lack of emotion was not very complimentary to John, but then found she could not bring herself to lay false claim to any feelings of great affliction. "I am very sorry, of course, that my father has had to suffer this grievous loss," she told him instead, "and, by the by, I should like to think you for your great kindness to him. As to the marriage," she continued in brisker accents, "it was an arrangement between our two families with which I was happy to comply—because I held your brother in great regard—but no more than that. He was aware of my feelings, but I was not entirely certain of his attitude to me." She dropped her voice a little at the end of this speech, amazed at her own temerity in talking like this to a man she had known scarcely two weeks; but she did not expect to see him again before they left the district.

"I cannot tell you how pleased I am to hear that that was the way of it," her companion said with surprising fervour. They had reached their destination now, and he held the door open and followed her into the posting-house.

Mr. Dorville was already there, seated at one of the tables, and Ann felt quite pierced by the look of despair on his face which quickly vanished when he saw their approach. He rose, picked up his gloves and stick, and came towards the young people.

"Well, sir, I have had a most enjoyable talk with your daughter and I am pleased to see she is taking this wretched business so well. How is Mrs. Dorville?" enquired his lordship kindly.

Mr. Dorville shook his head. "Very cut up, my Lord. But then so are we all. It will be a great wrench to leave the Grange."

"Leave the Grange!" echoed his lordship, looking stricken. "But you said nothing of this," he protested to Miss Dorville, in tones bordering on the accusatory.

"I've just this afternoon seen the agent who is quite sanguine about finding us a tenant," Mr. Dorville told them both, with no evident satisfaction. "It only remains for us to find an alternative lodging. Now, my lord, you must excuse us. I'd like to get home before the night closes in. I fear we may be in for some more snow." He proffered a hand to Lord Branthorpe, who gripped it in a stunned fashion.

When his lordship took leave of Miss Dorville he said urgently: "I shall see you before you go, of course. You must come to a small betrothal celebration we shall be having in the next day or two—if my traveller arrives safely today, that is," he finished and immediately seemed to regret his clumsiness, but Ann smiled in a mechanical fashion and made haste to follow her father to the stables.

The Earl's emblazoned coach stood in the yard, and as Ann gave it a last woe-begone look from their own carriage, his lordship would scarcely have said now that she was taking things well. His closing remarks had thrown a blight over the already gloomy prospect before her; she could only assume that he was waiting to collect his future bride, and that an invitation to their betrothal party was to provide her last sight of him. She would not go, of course, and although curious to see the lady she was not sorry that they pulled away before the London coach had arrived. That Miss Merivale was evidently not the Earl's choice was small consolation. Clearly, now that he had taken over his inheritance, Branthorpe would be anxious to marry. It was difficult to hazard his age, she mused, for his features were still fine-drawn from his sojourn abroad, but she thought he must be nearing thirty. She felt a sudden pang as she remembered their light-hearted references to his rather haggard appearance, on their ride together.

Wrenching her thoughts from this painful direction, she surprised her morose father by asking how quickly they would be able to move, and whether it would not be a good idea if he were to leave the following day to search at once for a new home.

* * *

The London Mail Coach, which set down its passengers only 200 yards from the Swan, was slightly late owing to one of the leaders going lame just past Tadcaster. Lord Branthorpe, whose mind was no longer on Mrs. Trant's arrival at all, was pacing up and down the cold street, anxious to be getting home, when he was startled by the Mail clattering over the cobbles accompanied by a great blast on the guard's horn. He wished he had been able to ensure, in his letter to Philip's mother, that she travel by hired post-chaise but, as he could scarcely involve her in such expense, he had recommended the Mail which he promised to meet. However, it was a sobering thought that if he had not arranged it so, he would most probably not have seen Miss Dorville before the whole family quit the Grange.

The sight of Mrs. Trant's squat figure, descending from the coach swiftly put his own worries from his mind, and he went forward to greet her with genuine pleasure. Her gentle brown eyes seemed in danger of starting from their sockets when she saw him.

"L-lord Branthorpe, well, I never. How good of you to arrange all this. How is my son?" she asked, anxiety suddenly added to her uncharacteristic air of distraction.

"No need to fret on that head, ma'am, he's in prime

twig again. Now, if you would like to walk a few yards to the Swan over there, I will have your boxes picked up and taken to my carriage." On hearing that she had only one modest-sized valise with her—which was all that was permitted on the Mail—he picked this up himself and carried it, which sent the good lady into a further twitter.

"You shouldn't, my lord, really," she protested. "I'm overjoyed to hear that Philip is better, of course, but it does mean you've been put to all this trouble for nothing, I fear," she chattered on, still agitated after the tiring journey and the unnerving transformation of poor, sick Mr. Frensham into the elegant noble lord striding along at her side carrying her valise.

"On the contrary, ma'am, your presence is still urgently needed at Branthorpe, but on a much more cheerful matter. Your son will explain when he sees you," Simon told her soothingly, although when he had sent for her on that first day of Philip's illness he had had no notion that things would fall out this way.

Seeing Mrs. Trant again had brought back very vividly to his mind the first dreadful days in England, together with the memory of her great kindness to him, and for the moment his present anxieties were forgotten. It was not until dinner that evening that he was able to consider again what was to be done about Miss Dorville.

Mrs. Trant had, by then, been joyfully reunited with her son who, although no longer bedridden, was still keeping to his room, and the two of them took dinner there together. This left the Dowager, Amelia and Simon to dine downstairs. Simon's announcement the previous day of Mrs. Trant's imminent arrival had been a complete surprise to them all as he had mentioned his letter to her to no one, until he was certain she could come. It was inevitable, therefore, that the first topic to be discussed over dinner was Philip's mother; Amelia seemed relieved that her future mother-in-law was both charming and understanding, for she had shown not the least censure on hearing their news and, indeed, was quite as eager as anyone to see her future grand-daughter the following day. It had been fixed that Philippa—or Mary Philippa, as she now was to be named, after Philip's first wife—should be collected from the gamekeeper's cottage then, and brought back to Branthorpe. Amelia and Betsy had been busy making ready the nursery, and Simon understood that there had been general rejoicing below stairs that the child was to return. He was gratified to see how exceedingly happy his sister looked this evening and had, perforce, to wait until this agreeable subject was exhausted before he could break the news of their neighbours' intention to leave the Grange, at which both ladies expressed their astonishment.

"Poor Ann!" cried Amelia. "Where will they go?"

"They seem all to pieces at the moment, and I would hazard they have no clear idea. But they seem resolved on moving quickly." He paused, then said to his sister: "I wondered if we might have them in to a small dinner party—to celebrate your betrothal, perhaps—before they go?"

Amelia looked doubtful. "I think we should do something, certainly, but I'm not sure Philip will be fit enough so soon. He is still quite weak, as you know. Could we not just invite them to a farewell dinner?" she suggested.

"We could," replied her brother, incidentally pleased to hear how readily Amelia referred to her fiancé as Philip, "but I fear they would decline in view of the awkwardness left by that abominable brother of ours." He explained to his sister that in spite of all his exhortations to John, he had merely left a note at the

Grange, as he rode out buoyantly to see Major Winthorpe again about the formalities involved in obtaining
a commission with his regiment.

The Dowager had been very pensive ever since hearing of the Dorville's impending move, and she ignored
these animadversions on her young son. "Simon," she
said, when her offspring was silent once more, "after
dinner you will be good enough to see Featherstone
and ask him to look out all the papers relating to the
Grange. I think they may provide interesting reading."

*   *   *

It occurred to Simon the next morning, as he rode
through a snow-storm of modest proportions to Shipton Grange, that his mother, once again, must have
divined his intentions. He wondered if she would have
drawn his notice to this particular clause in the Grange
lease if she had not wanted the Dorvilles to stay there
for some particular reason. Perhaps he was crediting
her, on this occasion, with more insight than was her
due, for she had never even seen her eldest son with
Miss Dorville in the way she had been able to observe
Mr. Trant's fondness of Amelia; but at least she had
provided Simon with an excuse to visit the Dorvilles at
once, and he gave thanks for that, whatever her motive
may have been.

Feeling distinctly like the wicked landlord of melo-
drama—but instead of turning the family into the snow
his endeavour was to keep them as neighbours at all
costs—he dismounted to open the Grange gate. He was
far from sanguine of the outcome of his visit, being un-
decided on whether to approach first the father, which
would be more punctilious, or the daughter, which appealed to him rather more.

When Prickett opened the door to him he found

himself asking to see Miss Dorville, presenting the excuse that he had a message from his brother. It was not until he was shown into the morning-room that he realised he had made the wrong choice, for Mrs. Dorville, whom he had inexplicably left out of his calculations, loomed large in the foreground ready to greet him, and her daughter was seated at a desk writing letters; both seemed thrown into confusion by his appearance.

"Lord Branthorpe! How kind in you to call in the circumstances," cried Mrs. Dorville in her customary sycophantic manner, but with a hint of tragedy subduing the performance this morning. "I'm sure we did not look for such complaisance, did we, my love?" she demanded of her discomfited daughter.

Ann left the bureau, greeted his lordship politely, and then all three stood about awkwardly until Simon found his voice. "I felt I had to call because I felt I left Miss Dorville under a misapprehension yesterday," he improvised hastily, and he noticed her attention quicken considerably at this remark, and it puzzled him slightly. "My sister's betrothal celebrations will not be able to take place as soon as I had hoped, and I thought I should let you know as soon as possible."

Ann, who had been unable to suppress an audible gasp of relief on hearing this news, looked astounded. "Your sister's betrothal? But I had no idea, I mean, I thought—. But this is splendid news? I am pleased," she said hurriedly, correcting herself.

His lordship, assuming that Miss Dorville had been a much closer friend of his sister's than he had realised, apologised. "I should have told you yesterday, but I own your news took me by surprise, and I didn't have time to explain everything. She is going to marry Mr. Trant, whom you met the other evening." He did not add that they were to live at Wragston Hall, fearing that this might throw Mrs. Dorville into strong hysterics.

"Oh yes, I remember, such a charming man!" said Mrs. Dorville automatically. "He is a nabob, too, I collect? But I can't bear to think of that happy occasion now. It is far too painful." She sank heavily into the nearest chair.

Ann gave her mother a quelling look, and enquired hastily about Mr. Trant's fever.

"Oh, he's vastly improved, thank you, but not sufficiently stout for a dinner party yet, which is the reason for the postponement." He turned to Mrs. Dorville and said earnestly: "I cannot tell you how sorry I am to hear of your decision to quit the Grange, ma'am, is it quite unavoidable?"

"Oh, absolutely! I couldn't countenance staying here, my lord, not now," she said pointedly and tight-lipped.

Simon noticed that Mrs. Dorville wore no token of mourning although he was touched to see that her daugher did still. He had to contrive, somehow, to speak to Miss Dorville alone, and was compelled to resort to the same device he had used, unnecessarily as it turned out, on the manservant for achieving this end; but with Mrs. Dorville he feared it might not succeed. "Would you permit me, ma'am," he began in his humblest manner," to have a few words with your daughter? I know you must think poorly of my brother, but this morning I am here as his emissary, and would be most grateful for the opportunity to make amends for some of the misunderstanding which must have arisen from his cursory line of conduct."

Mrs. Dorville gave the Earl a calculating look. "You are not saying I collect, that he had changed his mind?"

"I fear not, ma'am," replied Simon.

"Hmph," grunted Mrs. Dorville doubtfully. "Well, I suppose if my daughter has no objections it is a reasonable enough request." Her hesitation in leaving Ann with the Earl was a clear indication of the severe blow her schemes had received in the last few days.

His lordship cast a speaking look in Miss Dorville's direction, knowing that she would not likely to believe he conveyed any message from John after their private conversation the day before.

"Oh, none whatever," Ann confirmed. "On the contrary, I am most intrigued, my lord," she said, with a faint smile.

Then, with a great rustling of silk, and considerable dignity Mrs. Dorville quit the room.

As soon as the door closed behind her, Simon said: "Forgive the slightest deception, Miss Dorville, I wanted to speak to you and this was the only way I could contrive it."

"I guessed it might be so. But if you are not here as John's emissary, in what guise do you come?" she asked lightly, but busy arranging the folds of her lilac sarsnet gown as she seated herself on the sofa.

Simon moved restlessly about the room and, against the background of eddying snow seen through the tall window, presented an agitated picture which contrasted with Ann's tranquil pose.

"In two roles, I suppose," he said eventually. "And if I fail in the first, I shall have no alternative but to assume the second." He observed her puzzled expression. "I'm sorry, I do not mean to talk in riddles, but your sudden decision to leave the Grange compels me to divulge my intentions much sooner than I had planned, and I find it difficult. The fact is I *am* here in my brother's stead, in one respect at least. Would you consider marrying me, Miss Dorville?" Having delivered himself successfully of this prime question after a somewhat garbled introduction, he came to a halt not two paces from her.

The snow continued to fall in unremitting silent flurries.

Ann's blue eyes were raised up to his in sheer astonishment, her lips slight parted. "But you c-couldn't," she managed to stammer at last.

Simon, who thought he had never seen anyone so beautiful, was quite held in thrall by her expression and found himself sitting beside her. He took up one of her hands. "You see, I love you—I have done from the moment I saw you laughing so entrancingly at that ridiculous dog." The slim hand was not withdrawn from his and although her gaze was fixed now, in a bemused fashion, on her other hand which rested on the arm of the sofa, he saw nothing in that countenance to discourage him. "I hope you are not going to say it is impossible in so short a space of time," Then, with sudden inspiration, he added: "After all, it does happen—witness my sister and Mr. Trant!"

She turned her face slowly towards him, and under the long dark lashes her eyes had never looked more brilliant. She shook her head wonderingly and smiled. "Oh, I know now that it does, but I never dared hope—" she began in a small voice.

This was too much for his lordship and, abandoning her hand, he tilted her chin towards him and kissed her tenderly on the lips. "My love," he murmured, swiftly encircling her with his arms, and she responded with a fervour which surprised and excited him. He scarcely noticed that the high starched points of his collar were sticking uncomfortably into his chin; and neither participant saw the door open and Mrs. Dorville's rounded eyes fix briefly upon them, before it closed unheard.

Presently, Simon's conscience smote him, and he

said: "I hope you don't imagine that I influenced my brother's decision in any way."

"I don't mind if you did," came the complacent response from the dark shining head resting on his shoulder. Ann looked up at him mischievously. "But what a blessing papa's bank failed!" she said, then all at once she became serious. "I may not have any dowry to speak of, you know! How can you consider offering for me?" she asked as if, only now, she was realising how improbable it all was; she tried to push him away.

His lordship resisted the attempt, unruffled. "I'm not marrying you for your dowry. We shall contrive well enough, I daresay. In any event, I meant what I said to your father about his bank—I doubt he will be ruined."

She seemed disposed to accept his word on all counts without demur. "And what, then, was your second role?" she asked suddenly.

"Oh yes," he said, wishing he had never mentioned it now. "It has no doubt slipped your father's mind, but there is a clause in the long lease he had from my father stipulating that any sub-letting must meet with his approval. So you see, as his heir, I could put endless obstacles in your way by rejecting all your prospective tenants as undesirable—as, of course, they would be in comparison with the present highly desirable ones."

"I see, but that sounds suspiciously like coercion to me, my lord," Ann said, in reproving accents, but the slight quiver of her lips did not escape her companion.

"I think you may be right," his lordship admitted ruefully. "It looked uncomfortably like that to me, too, and I'm glad I shall not have to resort to such low stratagems. But I was quite determined you should not be allowed to escape." He kissed her lightly on the forehead. "Your mama will allow herself to be persuaded to stay, I fancy, in the light of these new circumstances."

"I imagine so," Ann replied in a failing voice.

"Now, I fear that lady will be returning at any moment to eject me, and you haven't answered my question yet—will you marry me, Miss Dorville?"

"I will, my lord, but on one condition," she said demurely.

"Which is?" Simon demanded with an anxious frown.

But Ann's eyes twinkled when they met his again. "That on no account will you buy me any more hunting prints."

"Or insist upon snails for dinner?" his lordship added gravely.